uncomfortable as Kirsten felt.

He wore his usual dark business suit, but his arrogant demeanor was gone.

Was he trying to soften the blow of a dismissal? she wondered.

Kirsten's hands tightened into fists. "Please, Mr. Forrester, if you're going to fire me, just say so. I can't stand the suspense any longer."

Court's eyes widened. "Fire you?" He found his voice. "Whatever gave you that idea?"

"What was I supposed to think when you summoned me to your office?"

"Good Lord." He took one of her trembling hands in his. "I just wanted to apologize for the other night. You wouldn't listen to me then, so I had to call and try again."

She could hardly believe what he was saying. "You mean you're not going to let me go?"

"Let you go?" His voice lowered. "Kirsten, my biggest problem right now is that I couldn't bring myself to let you go even if I wanted to."

Dear Reader,

Welcome to Silhouette—experience the magic of the wonderful world where two people fall in love. Meet heroines that will make you cheer for their happiness, and heroes (be they the boy next door or a handsome, mysterious stranger) who will win your heart. Silhouette Romance reflects the magic of love—sweeping you away with books that will make you laugh and cry, heartwarming, poignant stories that will move you time and time again.

In the coming months we're publishing romances by many of your all-time favorites, such as Diana Palmer, Brittany Young, Sondra Stanford and Annette Broadrick. Your response to these authors and our other Silhouette Romance authors has served as a touchstone for us, and we're pleased to bring you more books with Silhouette's distinctive medley of charm, wit and—above all—*romance*.

I hope you enjoy this book and the many stories to come. Experience the magic!

Sincerely,

Tara Hughes
Senior Editor
Silhouette Books

PHYLLIS HALLDORSON

Ageless Passion, Timeless Love

Silhouette *Romance*

Published by Silhouette Books New York

America's Publisher of Contemporary Romance

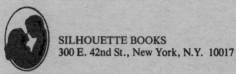

SILHOUETTE BOOKS
300 E. 42nd St., New York, N.Y. 10017

ISBN: 0-373-08653-9

First Silhouette Books printing June 1989

Printed in the U.S.A.

PHYLLIS HALLDORSON

At age sixteen Phyllis Halldorson met her real-life Prince Charming. She married him a year later, and they settled down to raise a family. A compulsive reader, Phyllis dreamed of someday finding the time to write stories of her own. That time came when her two youngest children reached adolescence. When she was introduced to romance novels, she knew she had found her long-delayed vocation. After all, how could she write anything else after living all those years with her very own Silhouette hero?

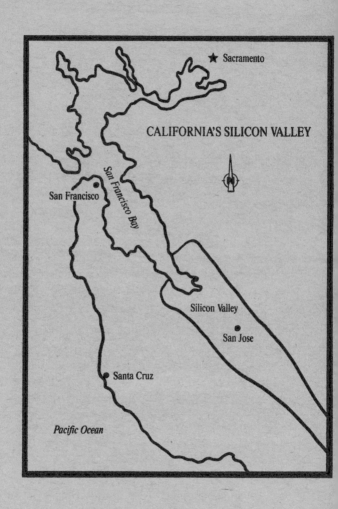

CALIFORNIA'S SILICON VALLEY

★ Sacramento

San Francisco

San Francisco Bay

Silicon Valley

San Jose

Santa Cruz

Pacific Ocean

Chapter One

Kirsten Anderson sat cross-legged on the thickly carpeted floor in the office of the personnel manager of Evergreen Industries and wrestled with the infant lying on a blanket in front of her. She was trying to fit a diaper on the bare bottom of the baby boy who was kicking vigorously and screaming at the top of his lungs.

She was definitely coming off second best. For twenty minutes she'd been in charge of this writhing bundle of rage, and already her blouse had pulled out of her skirt, the skirt was twisted and her brown hair was thoroughly disheveled.

"Jimmy, for heaven's sake, quiet down," she said, knowing that even if he could have understood her he couldn't have heard over the racket he was making. "How do you expect me to fit you into this if I can't even catch you?"

She grabbed again for his ankles, but he foiled her by rolling onto his stomach and turning up the volume of his outrage. Thank God it was Friday. In just two more hours she could go home, take a long, hot bath and forget about Evergreen Industries and her duties as mother confessor, financial consultant, referee and part-time babysitter; all came under the title of assistant manager in the personnel department.

She didn't hear the door open, and jumped when a male voice shouted into the din, "What in hell is going on here?"

Kirsten looked up and saw a tall, muscular man standing in the doorway. He was dressed in a khaki shirt with matching pants tucked into the tops of his laced-up boots, and his hair had the mussed look that removing a hard hat would have given it. "What's that child doing here, and where's Marguerite?" he demanded.

She picked up the half-nude infant and put him over her shoulder. He immediately stopped squalling and hiccuped. Marguerite Xavier was the personnel manager, and the man was a stranger, although he looked familiar. He was probably one of the construction workers who were building the new wing onto the electronics plant.

"Jimmy belongs to an employee on maternity leave," Kirsten explained. "She stopped by to get some information she needs for her medical insurance, and Marguerite took her over to the dispensary."

Kirsten clutched the baby to her shoulder with one arm, and with the other hand she awkwardly gathered up the blanket and diaper and tried to stand. The man reached down and put both hands under her arms and lifted her. He was strong, and his clothes were dusty and spotted with bits of cement and dirt.

"I gather you're the babysitter?" he said, and grinned as his gaze lit on the tiny bare buttocks that she cradled in her hand.

"I guess you could say that," she replied, and dropped the blanket and diaper on Marguerite's smooth desk top.

He laughed, and the sound was full-throated and playful. "You're awfully trusting," he said. "Haven't you learned yet that when left undiapered, baby boys can do unspeakable things to pretty dresses?"

As if on cue Kirsten felt the warm flow of moisture spreading down the bodice of her peach silk blouse. "Oh, no!" she moaned, and felt the flush of embarrassment color her creamy complexion. She held the small bundle away from her and looked down at the large stain that darkened the delicate material.

The man's laughter stopped abruptly, and he put out his arms. "Here, let me have him. If you're going to be a nursemaid you'd better learn how to put on a diaper."

She didn't correct his mistaken assumption about her profession but handed him the squirming child.

He took the infant and cradled him in his right arm while he spread the blanket on the desk with the other hand. Kirsten watched, beguiled, as he laid the baby on the blanket and reached for the diaper, all the while murmuring silly little nursery rhymes.

With the expertise of a man who had done it many times before, he made the little one squeal with laughter as he slid the diaper in place and taped it securely. "There you go, pal," he said, and again cradled little Jimmy in his arms as he turned to face Kirsten.

He seemed totally at ease, and his handsome face lit up with pleasure as he played finger games on the gurgling youngster's tummy, chest and neck. "You're obviously not a novice," she said. "How many children do you have?"

"Two, but they're well past the diaper stage. Haven't had a little one to play with in quite a while. Guess now I'll have to wait for grandchildren."

He looked too young to be talking about grandchildren, probably mid-thirties, although there were traces of gray in his dark, tousled hair. He wasn't wearing a wedding ring, but people who worked with construction equipment usually didn't wear jewelry due to safety precautions.

Kirsten sighed. "Yes, I suppose big families are rare nowadays. Few couples can afford more than two kids when the price of raising them keeps going up."

The glow faded from his face, and sadness replaced his laughter. "That's true, but it's too late for me, anyway. My wife died."

Kirsten felt a wave of compassion. "Oh, I'm so sorry," she said in a voice that was little more than a whisper.

He shrugged. "Yeah, so am I." He straightened up and handed her the baby. "Look, I don't have time to wait around. I'll drop by later to see Marguerite."

"But..." Kirsten started to protest as she took Jimmy from him.

"You'll do okay, honey, just hang in there," he said encouragingly. "You better practice that diapering, though, or the next time you may get a spray right in the face."

Before she could answer he was gone, and they hadn't even exchanged names.

All weekend Kirsten was disturbed by recurring thoughts and images of the ruggedly handsome man with the strong paternal instinct and the alternately happy and sad facial expressions. She had no idea who he was, and Marguerite hadn't known either when Kirsten described him to her. Marguerite had no appointments scheduled for that time, and the description hadn't rung a bell.

Back at work on Monday morning, an apprehensive Kirsten shifted on the comfortable chair in the tastefully decorated room and glanced at her watch. She'd been sitting in Courtney Forrester's outer office for half an hour, and it was now twenty minutes past the time scheduled for her appointment.

She'd twiddled her thumbs in doctors' and dentists' offices longer than that on many occasions. Still, she hadn't expected the big boss to keep one of his employees waiting when he was paying her to see that things ran smoothly in the personnel department of his electronics firm.

The tension she'd hoped to avoid built with every passing minute, and she ran her hand lightly over the brown, feathery bangs that teased the brow of her oval face. It was strictly a nervous gesture since she'd stopped in the restroom earlier to comb her hair and make sure the new navy-blue suit she'd worn for the occasion was unwrinkled and spotless.

She shuddered as she thought of the rumpled mess she must have looked on Friday when the stranger burst into Marguerite's office and found her cavorting around on the floor with the howling baby. No wonder he'd run off so quickly without even bothering to ask her name.

It was probably the first time since she'd started to work that she'd been less than fastidious in the office. She wore designer suits, feminine but beautifully tailored, styled her hair in a becoming but professional manner and behaved like a lady at all times.

A small groan escaped her. Why had the sexiest man she'd ever encountered picked the one time when she looked and behaved like a frumpy babysitter to make an entrance?

The receptionist looked up, and Kirsten managed to smile and pull her thoughts back to the problem at hand. In the four years she'd worked for Evergreen Industries, she'd never met the brilliant entrepreneur who, in his late twenties, had put together one of the first personal computers while working in his attic. Starting with nothing but an idea and a genius for marketing, Court Forrester had made Evergreen a household word and built the largest and most successful electronics firm in California's booming, high-tech Silicon Valley.

He was still only in his early forties, but Evergreen rated as a Fortune 500 company, and Mr. Forrester was listed as one of the fifty most influential men in America. Known as a fair but exacting employer, he had definite, and sometimes inflexible, ideas as to how he did and did not want his business run.

Not only was he rich and successful, but also handsome as a movie star. He was great copy for the television and newspaper photographers, and was often in the news. Kirsten had sighed along with every other woman between the ages of fifteen and death over grainy newspaper pictures of the dashing widower escorting various beautiful women to the glamorous cultural events in San Jose and nearby San Francisco.

Court Forrester was a formidable personality, and Kirsten was beginning to wish she'd appointed someone else to plead this cause that was so important to the efficiency and peace of mind of a majority of her co-workers.

Her nerves were strung so tightly that she jumped when the attractive young receptionist called her name. "Mr. Forrester will see you now," she said, and rose to escort Kirsten into the inner office.

The man behind the desk came forward and greeted her in a rich baritone voice. "Ms. Anderson, I'm so sorry to keep you waiting, but I was taking an overseas call."

Shock rocked through Kirsten, and all she could do was stare. Although today he wore a custom-made gray three-piece business suit and no one would ever mistake him for a laborer, Courtney Forrester was the charismatic man who had come to the personnel office on Friday!

No wonder he'd looked familiar.

For a moment he seemed puzzled by her reaction. Then he recognized her, too. He blinked and looked again, a classic double take. "*You* are Kirsten Anderson, our assistant personnel manager?'' He sounded as shocked as she felt.

She spoke the only words that came to mind. ''Oh my God!''

For a moment they just stood staring at each other. Finally Court broke the silence with a laugh of genuine amusement. ''Okay, so I mistook you for a nursemaid. Who did you think I was?''

''One of the construction workers,'' she said, and dared to smile.

This time they both laughed as he reached out his hand and she put hers in it. His was large and warm and strong. The hand of a determined, self-confident man.

The hand of a tender but passionate lover.

Kirsten quickly banished that transient, undisciplined thought.

''A natural mistake,'' he assured her. ''I'd just come from touring the construction site. I put myself through college by working summers in the building trade, and I loved it.'' For a moment he was thoughtful. ''Sometimes I wish I'd stayed with it. Everything was much simpler then.''

Kirsten was almost certain that this wasn't something he confessed to just anyone, and the counselor in her nature took over. ''I don't think you really mean that, Mr. Forrester,'' she said softly. ''It's not a small thing to be the first man to perfect the personal computer. You've earned a place in history.''

He squeezed her hand. ''That's very kind of you, and I wouldn't trade places with anyone. I can't help wishing that some things had turned out differently, though.''

For a few unguarded seconds her gaze roamed over him. He was tall, about six feet, and he had the build of a much younger man, lean and firm with muscles he didn't get by sitting behind a desk all day.

Maturely handsome, his square jaw indicated a genuine tenacity, but his gentle mouth promised unrestrained delights without ever saying a word.

Again Kirsten banished the unsettling thoughts. *Careful, girl. He's the big boss, the CEO, for heaven's sake.*

Her hand still rested in his, and the contact sent tingles all the way up her arm. For a moment, as their gazes met, his expressive brown eyes seemed to delve past her shaky defenses and ferret out her secret desires.

The magnetism between them lasted only a moment before it was abruptly cut off as he spoke. "Please, Kirsten, sit down."

He seated her in front of the desk, then returned to his chair behind it. His tone was friendly but impersonal when he spoke again. "Would you like some coffee?"

So much for her silly fantasizing. "No, thank you," she answered, and managed to make her tone equally impersonal.

"Then suppose you tell me what I can do for you."

His brown eyes were flecked with green, and his black hair was winged with silver at the temples. If possible, he was even better looking in person than in his pictures.

With difficulty Kirsten pulled her attention back to what she'd come for, then took a deep breath and plunged ahead. "I'm here to talk to you about a problem that is becoming more and more widespread, and also about a proposed solution."

Court frowned. "I wasn't aware that there was a problem in personnel."

"Oh, no, sir. It's not just confined to one area, it affects the whole plant. I'm referring to the difficulty so many of our workers have finding reliable and affordable child care."

"Child care?" He looked perplexed. "What do I have to do with child care?"

"Nothing. That is, everything." Oh darn, this wasn't going well at all. Kirsten could feel her self-confidence draining away, and fought to maintain it. "Look, Mr. Forrester, most of the people employed in Silicon Valley are young, twenties and thirties, and a lot of them have small children. Those youngsters need to be taken care of while their parents work."

"Now just a minute." He sounded annoyed. "I don't see where that's any of my—"

"Please," she interrupted, "let me finish. You were probably going to say this isn't something that affects you, but it does. Do you have any idea how many man-hours are lost by employees who have to stay home for a day or more because their babysitter moved out of the area or just didn't show up? How many trained women have to quit working after their babies are born because none of the day-care centers will take infants? Or how many emergency leaves are taken because a child is ill and no care-giver will take a sick child?"

"No," Court grated, "but I have a feeling that you're going to tell me."

Now Kirsten was getting annoyed. He wasn't taking her seriously. She sat up even straighter and recited the figures she'd memorized, the statistics that evidenced an appalling lack of care providers for the children of working mothers. "More than half of married women with children under age six are now employed," she concluded. "And that doesn't include the unmarried mothers. Research has shown that these women are more successful on the job if they know their children are well taken care of."

Court had leaned back in his chair. "All right," he said. "You've obviously studied this thoroughly, and I agree that there is a problem, but why are you bringing it to me? We've always had a liberal leave policy. I've never objected if parents want to use part of their sick leave to care for a family member who is ill. We also allow them to use their annual vacation time as they see fit, so staying home for a babysitting emergency shouldn't be a hardship.''

"We're all well aware of the excellent benefits the company provides," Kirsten assured him anxiously. "Believe me, sir, no one is complaining."

"Then why are you taking up my time? You don't have children, do you, Kirsten?"

She shook her head. "No, I don't."

"Then if this isn't a problem with you, how did you get involved, and what do you expect me to do?"

She relaxed a little. "I got involved because it's been brought to the attention of the personnel office that absenteeism is becoming a real problem. When I investigated I found that it's not only illness, or even goofing off, that's causing people to take unscheduled leave. A large number of both men and women are late or don't show up at all because of babysitting difficulties. This slows down work in all departments, and eventually interferes with our production schedules. It's not just the parents' problem; it affects the business, as well."

Court was silent for a moment. "If this is actually causing a slowdown in getting the work out, then something will have to be done about it. I assume you have a suggestion?"

Kirsten tensed again. Courtney Forrester seemed like a reasonable man, but what she was about to propose was still quite radical. An elusive intuition warned her that he wasn't going to be as enthusiastic as she was.

"Once I became aware of this development, I got together with some of the supervisors. After a lot of study we came up with a recommendation."

He said nothing, just looked at her with a probing gaze that told her to get on with it.

She took a deep breath. "Mr. Forrester, we feel that you could reduce absenteeism, increase production and cut the personnel turnover substantially if you'd set up a day-care center for infants and preschool children in the new wing that's being added to the plant."

That got his attention. His laid-back attitude disappeared as he sat up straight and glared at her. "Ms. Anderson, have you any idea what a project like that would cost?"

Kirsten was prepared for that question and tried not to cringe. "Yes, sir. I have all the figures here."

She thumbed through the report she'd brought, then stood and laid it on his desk, pointing to the relevant subcategory. "Here you are, the amount of space required, the cost of modifying existing plans, of setting up, of hiring qualified help. We realize that it would initially be very expensive, but it should eventually be self-supporting. Meanwhile, savings in lost man-hours and personnel turnover will offset the cost."

Court looked up at her and sighed. "Please sit down, Kirsten. I want to acquaint you with a few home truths. I'm a businessman. My responsibility to my employees includes providing a fair wage scale, a safe workplace and pleasant working conditions. Evergreen goes beyond that. We offer a choice of free medical insurance, up to four months of paid maternity leave, a fully equipped health club in the basement and limited resources to help employees with personal problems that affect their ability to do their jobs."

He stood and leaned over the desk. "*Limited* resources, Kirsten, and that does *not* include raising children. If parents can't take care of their own babies, then they have no business having them."

She couldn't believe what she was hearing. "B—but you like children . . ."

She'd been so impressed with the patient way he'd handled little Jimmy on Friday. He was a natural father, and he'd made no attempt to hide his pleasure in tending to the baby.

"Of course I do," he said. "That's why I don't like the idea of parents having them and then turning them over to some stranger whose main interest is not the child but how much money it will bring in."

"Mr. Forrester—"

He held up his hand as he interrupted her. "I listened to you, now do me the courtesy of hearing me out. If a woman wants a career, fine, but having a family today is largely a matter of choice, and a woman who chooses to have babies should be willing to stay home and take care of them."

Kirsten was appalled by this man's outdated and chauvinistic views about a woman's place, but she managed to control her anger and speak calmly. "Mr. Forrester, I'm sorry, but I have to disagree with you. Surely you're aware that few families can survive on one income in today's economy. Even if they could, a woman deserves the same opportunity as a man to make use of her talents and interests."

Court sat down again and toyed with a pencil. "I couldn't agree more. You've been working here for several years; you must be aware that I've always been an equal-opportunity employer. Women are as essential in the workplace as men. However, that doesn't change the fact that children have to be nurtured, and it's the parents' privilege and responsibility to do it."

Kirsten was becoming thoroughly exasperated. "I agree, but they don't have to be with them twenty-four hours a day."

"Yes, they do, or at least a big part of it. An infant needs constant care, and the first few months are crucial. That's when they bond with the mother, and that bonding is important for both mother and child."

"Yes, but—"

"I have two children," he continued, as though she'd never spoken. "A daughter and a son, and my wife was a full-time mother. She was always there when they needed her. She saw them take their first steps, heard them say their first words, was at home to supervise them after school. She breast-fed them for the first year, nursed them through illnesses and did double duty in Cub Scouts and Brownies when the working mothers couldn't fulfill their obligations."

Kirsten was again on her feet. "Now wait just a minute, dammit! That's not fair!"

It crossed her mind that this was her boss she was talking to, and she could lose her job if she wasn't careful, but outrage overcame caution. "I'm sure your wife was the perfect mother, but comparing her to women on the assembly line is like comparing computers with upright typewriters. Your family income was probably more in a week than theirs is in a year. Mrs. Forrester didn't have to worry about putting a roof over her children's heads and food in their stomachs."

"The hell she didn't," Court roared, as he, too, got to his feet. "I was only a few years out of college, which I'd attended on scholarships and loans. I had a mountain of debts to repay on the slave wages I received at the electronics firm where I was a new employee. We lived in a small two-bedroom house in the cheap-rent district, and I drove our only car to work. Barbara knew fifty different ways to cook hamburger, and she planted a garden and canned her own vegetables."

"Oh." He'd taken the steam out of Kirsten. She'd read the articles about him. She should have remembered that he'd started the business on a shoestring.

"I haven't always been successful, young lady," he continued, less belligerently. "In those days I worked all day and spent half the night in the attic trying to work out plans for a small, uncomplicated computer. We never got through a whole month without running out of money. If it hadn't been for Barb's garden and the orange tree in the backyard, we'd probably have gone hungry once in a while."

Kirsten sat back down and so did Court. She wondered what he'd been like as an underpaid and overworked young husband. Tenacious and headstrong, surely. She didn't have to know him well to recognize that he still had those qualities in abundance.

He'd probably been passionate, too, but a controlled passion. After his lecture on family planning she'd bet his own children had come along by design rather than by accident.

He still radiated a sexual vitality that made her wonder what it would be like to break through that control and receive the full force of his desire.

She shivered slightly and pulled her attention back to the present. He was apparently waiting for her to respond to his tirade. "I'm sorry," she said quietly. "I apologize for making unwarranted assumptions. You mentioned on Friday that you had children, but I thought you meant small ones. How old are they now?"

He smiled. "Noelle is about your age, maybe a little younger. She's twenty-one and a senior at San Jose State. John is nineteen and a sophomore at Yale."

Kirsten chuckled. "You're not old enough to be my father," she said, and wondered why it was so important to her that he know she was older than his daughter. "I'm twenty-five and I graduated from U.C. Santa Cruz four years ago. I've been working here ever since."

"And doing an excellent job, I'm told," he said appreciatively, then changed the subject. "Do you mind if I ask you a personal question?"

She was startled enough to stammer, "Why . . . why no."

"What are your long-range goals? Do you plan to marry and have a family, or are you going to concentrate on your career?"

She was caught off guard, and it took her a moment to reply, "It never occurred to me that I'd have to make a choice. Of course I want a husband and children. I come from a large and loving family, and I want to continue that life-style with one of my own, but that doesn't mean I can't have a career, too."

"Then you plan to return to work as soon as possible after your babies are born? May I ask who's going to raise them?"

He was throwing questions at her too fast. She couldn't think straight. "*I'll* raise my babies. Or rather, their father and I will."

He quirked one eyebrow. "You intend to marry a man who's unemployed?"

"No, of course not," she snapped.

"Then how do you expect to nurture your little ones if both you and this mythical husband are away from them all day?"

Again Kirsten jumped to her feet, but this time she turned her back on her employer and walked across the room. For the first time she realized that she'd never thought about what she'd do after she had children. She'd always figured there would be time enough to worry about that once she found a man she wanted to marry.

"I didn't say I'd go back to work immediately after my babies were born. I'd probably ask you for an extended leave of absence so I could be with the child for the first year."

"I wouldn't grant it, you know." His tone was cold. "I have a business to run. If I didn't need someone here, every day, to do your job, I wouldn't have hired you in the first place."

His words stung, and she whipped around to face him. "Then I'd quit! I'm well educated and efficient. I could get another job when I decided to go back to work again."

He came from behind the desk and walked over to her. "What you're saying is that you agree with me, an infant needs its mother, or father, with it during its formative years."

Kirsten was furious. He was putting her on the spot, then twisting her answers to suit himself.

"You've got me so confused that I don't know what I'm saying," she snapped.

"Then maybe you should think about it before you come in here and tell me that an employer should not only take care of his employees, but their children, as well. Barbara and I did without many of the things most people consider necessities, but we were happy and our children were secure in the knowledge that they were loved and properly cared for."

He moved away from her and stood looking out the window at the city of San Jose spread out below. "When a man and woman decide to have a baby they give up the freedom to think only of their own wants and needs. They should be willing to sacrifice some things if necessary so that one of them can stay home and raise the child."

At least he's willing to include men in the nurturing process, Kirsten observed, but she was still upset by his all-knowing attitude about what women should and should not do.

She cleared her throat. "All right, since it seems to be so important to you, I'll agree that it would be beneficial if a mother could spend full time with her preschool children. Would you be willing to give your employees of either gender a five-year leave of absence, with pay, of course, so that would be possible?"

Kirsten knew she was on dangerous ground, taunting the boss like that, but she couldn't resist. He simply refused to face the facts as they were instead of as he'd like them to be. Just because his wife was willing to live in poverty didn't mean all women were.

Court turned around, and this time she could see that she'd gone too far. His features were twisted, and his eyes were cold.

"If you have nothing better to do than mock me, Ms. Anderson, then I think you'd do well to get back to your desk and find something. I'm not interested in setting up a child-care center on the premises, and that's my final decision. Goodbye."

He strode back to his desk and left her standing there, looking stunned.

Chapter Two

Kirsten spent the afternoon in a haze of conflicting emotions, alternately damning Courtney Forrester as a chauvinist and castigating herself as a clumsy fool.

How could she have been so childish as to engage in a game of one-upmanship with the man she needed so desperately to impress with her maturity and good sense?

She snorted inelegantly. Good sense? She'd been so far out of her league it had been laughable. He'd been in charge from the minute she'd walked into his office. First tantalizing her with his charm, then confusing her with his quick, angry response to her proposal, and finally goading her into losing her temper.

Good grief, after all her research, her conferences with architects, child-care licensing bureaus and the fire, health and sanitation departments, she'd blown the whole thing by taking up the battle for women's rights instead of gently pointing out the errors in his cherished "home truths."

She gave up trying to concentrate on the figures she was preparing for the finance department. Now what was she going to do? She couldn't just drop this idea; it was too important. She and her committee had put too much time into it to give up just because she couldn't control her temper.

Maybe she could get Marguerite Xavier, the personnel manager, to intercede. Marg would have more influence with Mr. Forrester than an assistant manager like herself.

Kirsten banished the thought immediately. No way. That would be admitting to both of her superiors that she'd failed in the assignment she'd been so eager to take on.

No, this was Kirsten's baby, so to speak, and it was up to her to give birth to it. She'd have to apologize—anything short of getting on her knees—and try to get Court Forrester to give her another chance to convince him that an on-site day-care center would be an excellent business investment.

She glanced at her watch. Four o'clock. An hour before quitting time. She picked up the phone and spoke to his receptionist. "Tanya, this is Kirsten. Look, I've got to see Mr. Forrester again. Is he still there?"

"Yes, but . . ." The skeptical voice on the other end hesitated.

"I know," Kirsten hastily inserted, "I'm not his favorite employee right now, but this is really important. If I come up could you get me in?"

"Gosh, Kirsten, I don't know. He's on the phone, and he's given orders that he's not to be disturbed."

"Do you know how much longer he'll be in the office?"

Again Tanya hesitated. "Well, he didn't say, but . . . Oh, wait, he just hung up. Do you want me to put you through?"

"No, I doubt if he'd see me if I asked. I'm coming right up. Just try to keep him available till I get there." She slammed down the receiver and headed for the elevator.

A few minutes later she walked into the chief executive officer's outer office with as much dignity as she could muster under stress. "Is he still here?" she asked anxiously.

Tanya laughed. "He's hardly had time to get from his desk to the door. What did you do, fly?"

Kirsten grinned. "I would have if I'd had the proper equipment. Look, I don't want to get you in trouble because of my pushy tactics. Isn't there something you could do in the empoyees' lounge for a few minutes?"

"Gotcha," Tanya said and winked. "I'll take a short break. But be forewarned. He's been testy ever since your visit this morning, so I wouldn't push him too far if I were you."

Tanya left and Kirsten walked over to the inner-office door and knocked.

"Yes, Tanya, come in," said a familiar voice from the other side.

Kirsten shut her eyes for a moment, then turned the knob and pushed the door open just far enough to peek around. "Sorry, Mr. Forrester," she said in her most placating tone. "There was nobody in the reception room so I knocked."

She entered the office and shut the door behind her.

Court looked startled, but then apparently remembered his manners and stood. "Kirsten. What brings you back? I thought we concluded our business this morning."

He didn't look very happy to see her, but neither was he still breathing fire and smoke. "No, sir. I mean, I'm sorry to barge in on you like this, but I couldn't leave without apologizing for my behavior. It was inexcusable, and I'm sorry."

His stern expression relaxed a little, and he came from behind the desk to stand in front of her. "I'm afraid I deserved your ire. I was being rude and insufferable, so let's call it a draw. If you'll accept my apology I'll accept yours."

"It's a deal," she said with a smile, and put out her hand.

He took it in his, and again she felt the warmth and strength that radiated from his touch. She wondered what it would be like to be held in his arms, then quickly switched thoughts as a wave of heat swept through her.

He didn't release her hand immediately, and she dared to hope that the contact was as pleasing to him as it was to her. Then he cleared his throat and let go of her.

He looked at his watch. "If that's all, I really am rather busy," he said pointedly.

Kirsten realized that she was about to botch the whole thing again, and immediately snapped to attention. "Please, could I just have a few more minutes? I'd like to try to convince you to give me another chance to explain how a day-care center could benefit you and your stockholders, as well as your employees."

She could see by his expression that he was about to refuse, and she hurried on. "I understand why you feel as you do. Apparently your wife had a deep maternal instinct and felt as strongly as you do that your children needed her at home."

A flicker of pain crossed his face and settled in his green-flecked brown eyes. "Yes, she did. Barbara was the kindest, most loving woman I've ever known. Her whole life centered around me and our son and daughter."

His shoulders slumped and there was a pinched look about his features. Kirsten was appalled to realize that she'd inadvertently reopened an unhealed wound and exposed a terrible vulnerability in this powerful man.

Without thinking, and acting only on a need to comfort, she put her hand on his arm. "I'm so sorry." Her tone echoed her distress. "You loved her very much, didn't you?"

He put his hand over hers and pressed it harder against him. "Very much," he confirmed.

The wool of his coat sleeve was spun fine and soft, but the muscles beneath it were hard.

"How long has she been gone?" Her gaze met his and clung.

"Three years." Their voices had become softer, more intimate, as the subject became more personal. "I've finally learned to live without her, but..." His words trailed off, and the sadness in his eyes receded as they roamed slowly over her upturned face. "Thank you for your understanding. You're very perceptive for one so young."

The magnetism between them was so strong that Kirsten had to use all her control not to lean toward him. When she felt his arms encircle her waist she knew he'd lost the same battle, and she relaxed and breathed a sigh as he drew her to him until their bodies were touching, but lightly.

He was amazingly gentle as he rubbed his cheek against hers and held her. She didn't recognize the elusive scent of his shaving lotion, but it had a sensual, expensive quality and she knew it would haunt her in the days to come. The muscles in his chest and waist were as firm as those in his arms, and when she put her arms around his neck she felt his shoulders ripple. He was solid, and she knew that he could crush her in the full force of unleashed passion.

She didn't dare speak or move for fear he'd come to his senses and put her away from him. Instead she contented herself with caressing the back of his neck and head with her fingers, soothing knotted muscles and tightened nerves.

It was the sharp ring of the telephone that broke the spell. They both jumped and sprang apart as the intrusive noise split the silence.

Court reached the desk in one stride while Kirsten turned away and walked to the window.

"Yes?" Court barked into the phone. He listened for several seconds, then said, "Tell him I'll call back in a few minutes," and hung up.

The silence that followed was leaden with tension, but now it was awkward and disconcerting rather than sensual. When Court finally broke it his voice was raspy. "My God, Kirsten, I'm sorry. I assure you I don't make a habit of...uh...coming on to young women. I don't know what I could have been thinking of."

Kirsten was shaken all the way to her navy-blue pumps, but she couldn't allow him to take all the blame. She clasped her hands together to keep them from shaking and turned to face him. "It was my fault as much as yours. I seem to have a habit of prying into personal areas of your life that are none of my business. Please forgive me."

He shook his head. "You have a loving and compassionate nature, and that's something you should be proud of, not apologize for. I took advantage of it. The responsibility is mine, and I promise it will never happen again."

He walked toward her but didn't get within touching distance. "You wanted to talk more about your proposal for a day-care center," he said, and once again his tone was all business. "I'm sorry, but I don't have the time right now. Check with Tanya on your way out and ask her to set up an appointment. I'd like to meet with your full committee next time if it can be arranged."

Kirsten recognized his reluctance to be alone with her again. She agreed that it would be unwise and unprofessional. All her instincts told her to get out of his office and forget she'd ever met him. To put someone else in charge of the day-care idea and catch up with all the other work on her desk, but she knew she wouldn't do that.

"Thank you," she said. "The committee would be pleased to meet with you anytime at your convenience."

As she walked out and closed the door behind her, she couldn't help but wish that the sexy construction worker she'd met on Friday had been exactly what he'd seemed to be. If he'd been middle-class, blue-collar Joe Blow, she was certain they'd have met again, and their relationship would have been special.

On the other hand, there was no future at all with Courtney Forrester, and only heartbreak and loneliness ahead if she ever made the mistake of dreaming that there could be.

The door closed behind Kirsten, and Court went back to his desk and sat down. He reached for the phone and noticed that his hand was shaking.

Damn. He hadn't been this unsettled by an encounter with a woman since he'd first met Barbara more than twenty years ago!

He pushed back his chair and strode across the room to the small corner bar where he poured a hefty portion of whiskey into a glass. Court had learned in the early months after Barbara's death not to drink alone. That was a seductive way to become an alcoholic, and he'd had two children to finish raising. Now, though, he needed to calm down and get back to work, and whiskey was a great stabilizer if you didn't overdo it.

He took the glass and stood looking out the window, but he wasn't seeing the busy streets of downtown San Jose. Instead he was seeing Kirsten as he'd first seen her, tumbling on the floor with a loudly protesting infant.

He'd mistaken her for college age with her tousled hair and disheveled clothes. Even so, he'd felt the pull of attraction, and had hastily dismissed it as fatherly admiration.

Fatherly admiration! *Oh, come on, Forrester, you know the difference between fatherly admiration and sensual attraction.* To be truthful, it wasn't either of those emotions he'd felt. It was something that transcended both—an affinity with her that had disturbed him as strongly as it had enticed him.

He'd quickly focused his attention on the baby in an effort to keep it off the girl and had taken the first opportunity to cut and run, certain that he'd never see her again.

Court took a long swallow of his drink. At first he hadn't recognized her when she'd walked into the office that morning. He'd seen a beautiful young woman with neatly styled hair the color of light chocolate and eyes to match. Kirsten Anderson had only been promoted to the rank of assistant manager of personnel a few months before, and he'd never met her. Although all the statistics on her background and education were available to him, he'd somehow formed a very different picture of his newest supervisor.

He'd been caught off guard by her fresh young loveliness, and the rounded womanly curves that couldn't be disguised by the softly tailored dress she wore. It wasn't until she reacted with such surprise when she saw him that he realized she was the same girl who had touched a nerve in him earlier.

Court took another drink of the whiskey. Only she wasn't a girl, she was a woman, and the last thing he'd expected was to find her cradled in his arms only hours later.

A muscle in his hand twitched involuntarily, sloshing the liquor around in the glass.

How in hell had that happened? Obviously it had been too long since he'd had a woman.

He frowned, remembering. No, it couldn't be that. Now that he thought of it, he hadn't even been aroused. It wasn't a passionate embrace, and yet it had affected him so deeply that he couldn't seem to pull himself together.

They'd been talking about Barbara, and that still had the power to upset him. It must have shown in his face, because she'd looked at him with such compassion before she touched him.

He hadn't even been aware of reaching for her until he was holding her. She'd felt so soft and warm in his arms, and her flawless cheek was smooth against his rougher one. He wasn't at all sure he could have forced himself to let her go if he hadn't been startled out of his enchantment by the telephone.

That thought upset him even more than the experience had.

The Saturday evening the Anderson family had been excitedly preparing for had finally arrived. The Crippled Children's Society was holding its annual awards banquet and Kirsten's father, Dane Anderson, was to receive the society's highest award for both financial contributions and volunteer service.

She drove her red sports car into the driveway of her parents' four-car garage and parked behind the area where her mother kept her Mercedes. Kirsten knew her dad would insist on taking Anderson Realty's company-owned limousine on this auspicious occasion.

She picked up her beaded bag and clutched her long green taffeta skirt as she slid out of the car and headed for the beautiful old hand-carved doors of the brick Tudor-style home that had been in her father's family for three generations.

She rang the bell and was greeted by Stella, the housekeeper, who had been the Anderson children's liberalized version of a nanny when they were growing up. "I'm glad you came early," she said. "Ruth Anne and your ma have locked horns, and neither of them is going to give an inch."

It was a familiar complaint. "Oh dear," Kirsten said as she handed Stella the angora stole she'd been wearing. "What's the problem this time?"

Stella took the wrap and folded it. "Ruth Anne's dress. You'd better get up there before they upset your dad."

Kirsten ran up the stairs and down the hall to her youngest sister's room. Even before she opened the door she heard her mother's raised voice. "I'm sorry, but I won't allow you to wear that outfit. It's too sophisticated for a child your age."

"Oh, Mother!" Ruth Anne wailed as Kirsten walked in.

"Are you two aware that you can be heard right through the closed door?" she said. "What's going on?"

Helen Anderson, looking far too glamorous in a designer gown to be a grandmother, sat stiffly on the ruffled calico spread of her youngest child's canopied bed. Ruth Anne, wearing a low-cut chiffon dress, was hunched on the vanity stool, looking mutinous.

"I'm giving your sister a choice of either changing her dress or staying home," Helen answered angrily.

"Then I'll stay home," Ruth Anne shouted and jumped to her feet.

"Whoa, now, calm down," Kirsten said as she crossed to where her sister stood. "Turn around and let me see."

The teenager pranced in a circle. The garment was black, a perfect showcase for her light blond loveliness. It was a little elegant for such a young girl, but certainly not worth making a fuss over in Kirsten's estimation.

"What's wrong with the dress?" she asked her mother.

"You know as well as I do what's wrong with it," Helen snapped. "It's cut all the way to the navel, and it's black. Young girls never wear black."

"Oh, Mother!" Ruth Anne wailed again.

Kirsten ignored the interruption. "Then why did you buy it for her?"

"Me buy it?" Helen raised her voice again. "I didn't even know she had it until just a few minutes ago. I thought she was going to wear this."

Helen picked up a dress from beside her on the bed and held it for Kirsten's inspection. It was pink with cap sleeves, a bodice that buttoned to the throat with tiny pink buttons and a flounce at the ankle.

"I bought it for her at Neiman-Marcus when I was in San Francisco last week," Helen continued.

"In the children's department," Kirsten guessed.

"Of course. She's not old enough for adult formals."

Ruth Anne groaned and burst into tears as she fled into the bathroom and slammed the door.

Kirsten walked over and sat down on the bed beside her mother. "Mom, Ruthie is sixteen years old. She's not a child anymore. She wouldn't even be able to button that dress. She wears the same size bra as I do."

Helen looked nonplussed. "Well, then, that's all the more reason for her not to flaunt herself in that black outfit. She's not even wearing a bra!"

Kirsten fought back a smile. "Are you?" she asked as her gaze roamed over the bare shoulders of her mother's teal-blue-and-metallic-silver gown.

"That's different," Helen retorted. "I'm an adult."

"And a very beautiful one," Kirsten said gently. "But you'd better start looking around you. Just be thankful that Ruth Anne isn't insisting on a miniskirt and green hair. I'm not kidding. Let her grow up, Mother. She's not your baby any longer."

Helen threw up her hands in defeat and retreated, turning her youngest daughter over to her eldest.

Kirsten and Ruth Anne went downstairs a few minutes later and joined their mother and father in the den. With the Andersons was their third daughter, Ingrid, a statuesque blonde, two years younger than Kirsten and the mother of their first grandchild.

Dane Anderson embraced Kirsten. "Sorry I wasn't around to greet you when you arrived, honey. I must have been in the shower."

He held her away from him and looked at her, his gaze taking in the low, square-cut neckline and full skirt of her emerald-green taffeta gown. "I'm going to be the envy of every man at the banquet tonight," he said huskily. "Who else can claim to have the four most gorgeous women in all of California?"

"No one," Kirsten teased, used to his extravagant flattery. "But when two such beautiful people as you and Mom team up, you can't help but produce ravishing daughters."

She wasn't exaggerating about her parents' looks. At forty-six, her mother, a partner in the legal firm of Guiley, Wilson, Anderson and Stoltenberg, was spectacular. Her figure was as good as her daughters', and her black hair, which tonight she wore piled high on her head, was thick and shining without a trace of gray. She looked ten years younger than she was.

Dane Anderson was forty-nine, six-foot-one, with a broad chest and slender waist. His eyes were sky blue, his hair only slightly darker than the honey blond it had been in his youth, and he looked smashing in his black tuxedo.

Together Dane and Helen were a stunning couple, and Kirsten adored them both.

When they arrived at the clubhouse they were surrounded by friends and well-wishers, but after a while Kirsten and Ingrid wandered out onto the deck overlooking the golf course to wait for the call to dinner. "It's too bad Ellery couldn't be here," Kirsten said.

"Yes," Ingrid agreed. "He really hated not getting to see Dad receive his award, but we just didn't feel right about leaving the baby."

"We all understand that," Kirsten assured her. "When do you think you'll be going back to work?"

Tall and willowy, with her father's and Ruthie's blond hair, Ingrid was the professional beauty of the family, a fashion model. "Not until I stop nursing that little butterball of mine," she said with a laugh. "I can't get back in shape while I'm eating for two."

Kirsten grinned. "You look in fine form to me."

"You don't see me the way the camera and the audience does. Every extra ounce and inch shows." She sighed. "Actually, I wouldn't be in any hurry to go back to work at all if we didn't need the money, but with mortgage payments, car payments and all the extra expense of raising a child . . . well, I don't really have a choice."

Kirsten could sympathize with her sister, who was torn between wanting to spend her time with her tiny daughter, and an equally compelling need to help provide a decent standard of living. In time her husband, a dentist, would be able to support his family without Ingrid's assistance, but for now he was just setting up a practice and their debts outweighed their income.

"I should get you to talk to my boss," Kirsten said. "Maybe you could penetrate his thick skull."

Ingrid's eyes widened. "You mean Courtney Forrester? Whatever for?"

Kirsten told her sister about the child-care project she was involved in, and Forrester's inflexible attitude toward it. She carefully left out the short but tender scene in his office, which had kept her awake most of the night fighting off yearnings and dreams that could never be fulfilled.

"I made an appointment for him to meet with my committee next Wednesday, but I don't have much hope that he'll change his mind," she concluded.

Just then dinner was announced, and the Anderson sisters headed for the banquet room.

Dane and Helen were seated at the head table, but their daughters sat with other family members toward the back of the room. Kirsten was busy talking to aunts, uncles and cousins during the meal and didn't pay any attention to the honorees and dignitaries on the dais at the front.

It wasn't until the last of the dessert dishes had been cleared away and the chairman had called for attention and introduced the master of ceremonies that she ended her whispered conversation with her aunt and focused her scrutiny on the people seated with her parents. Even though the rest of the large room was dimly illuminated with decorative candelabras on the tables, lights above the dais had now been turned on so that the people seated there could more easily be seen.

Her mouth dropped open with shock as her gaze rested on the man standing at the lectern. It was Court Forrester!

He was dressed neither as a laborer nor a businessman, but she'd recognize the commanding man in the tuxedo anywhere. She couldn't mistake the wings of silver at the temples that highlighted his thick raven hair. Or the boldly handsome features that would have made him a success as a male model had he been so inclined.

Court was a talented public speaker. He was both humorous and serious as he introduced the honorees, gave a touching sketch of why each was being honored and presented the plaques. Kirsten's admiration for him grew, and she wondered if there was anything he couldn't do well. If only he didn't have such a blind spot where working mothers were concerned.

The highest award was presented at last, and as Dane Anderson rose to receive it the applause was thunderous. As the son of a pioneer family and owner, along with his brother and sister, of a large, multigenerational real estate business, he was well-known and liked in San Jose's business and social communities. Helen was also introduced, but it was only mentioned in passing that they had three daughters.

Afterward there was dancing and Kirsten had no lack of partners. Although she saw Court watching her at times and smiled at him, he neither smiled back nor acknowledged her presence. Unable to believe he was deliberately snubbing her, she decided that he didn't recognize her in all her finery. Tonight she wore her hair swept back and pinned with orchids as opposed to her usual modified bouffant style, and she certainly didn't wear low-cut formal gowns in the office.

Finally she decided to approach him. She wanted to tell him how much she and the rest of the family had appreciated his glowing words of praise for her father when he'd presented Dane with the award.

She watched and waited until he was alone, then made her way across the room to where he stood. Her glance caught his as she moved closer, but although their gazes held he still didn't answer her wide smile or take a step in her direction.

A feeling of anxiety crept along her nerve ends. She knew he recognized her now, so why was he acting so cool?

He didn't speak until she was standing directly in front of him, and when he did his tone was icy. "Well, Kirsten, this is a surprise. I don't remember seeing you here at the country club before."

Up close he looked even more elegant and sophisticated in his evening clothes, and his words were friendly enough. Maybe he was just tired. "Hello, Mr. Forrester," she said after a pause that was a few seconds too long. "No, I haven't—"

"How did you find out I'd be here?" he interrupted impatiently. "Did you see my name in the newspaper accounts of the ceremony, or is there someone at work who gives you information about my schedule?"

Kirsten's bewilderment changed to indignation. "I don't know what you're talking about," she said stiffly. "I had no idea you'd be here."

"Oh, come now, aren't you being a little obvious?" he taunted. "You want something from me, and what better way to soften me up than by getting on a friendly basis socially?" He made no further attempt to hide his anger. "No doubt it would work on a younger, less jaded man, but you're wasting your time trying it on me. Frankly, I thought you were too intelligent to attempt such a maneuver.''

Kirsten could feel the flush that stained her cheeks, but before she could answer, her father called to her. ''Kirsten, there you are.'' He walked over to where she stood and recognized Court. ''Oh, Court, sorry, I didn't mean to interrupt. I see you already know my daughter, which is hardly surprising since she works for you.'' He turned his attention back to Kirsten. ''Are you about ready to leave, honey? Ingrid wants to get home in time to give the baby her one o'clock feeding, and your mother and I don't like the idea of sending her alone in a cab.''

Kirsten had been watching Court, and she gleefully saw his shock and discomfiture. It served the pompous ass right. She couldn't have thought of a better retort than her father's unconscious put-down.

''She's *your daughter*?'' Court nearly choked on the words.

Her father looked confused. ''Why, yes, our eldest. I'm sorry, I thought you two were talking when I came over. Kirsten and her two sisters, being the loyal daughters that they are, came with us tonight to see me get my award.''

Kirsten watched the color that had drained from Court's face rush back with a surge of embarrassment, but instead of the triumph she'd expected to relish, she encountered a dismaying twinge of sympathy that pricked at her heart. Courtney Forrester didn't deserve her empathy. He'd brought it all on himself by being so egotistical.

''Kirsten, I…I'm sorry…'' he stammered, but she turned to her father and spoke before Court could continue.

''I'm ready to leave anytime you are, Dad,'' she said. ''I'll go find Ruth Anne and meet the rest of you at the car.''

She walked away without a word or a glance for Court.

Chapter Three

It was ten minutes after six on that late October Sunday morning, and the first fingers of dawn were poking their way through the darkness. Courtney Forrester watched from his glass-enclosed breakfast room as the streaks of light grew broader and longer against the clear sky.

Even after twelve years of meals in this room he still felt like a bird on display in one of those fancy glass cages. The whole damn house was glass, and he'd never gotten used to the loss of privacy, the feeling of being watched from behind every bush or tree, that so much exposure had afflicted him with.

When he'd objected during the time the architect was drawing up the plans, Barbara had pleaded with him. "Oh, please, Court. After all those years of run-down little shacks in trashy neighborhoods, I just can't believe that we're going to have acres of lawns, gardens and trees all to ourselves. I want to be able to see it from anywhere in the house."

Court sighed as the memory brought with it a special sadness. He hadn't denied her the many-windowed walls.

It wasn't the memory of his wife that was tormenting him now, though. It was the puzzled hurt on the exquisite face of Kirsten Anderson, and his guilty conscience, that had made him toss and turn all night.

He's made a jackass of himself, but that was nothing new. He'd done it before. However, it had never bothered him as badly as it did now. Usually when it happened he apologized and put it behind him after making a mental note to be more careful in the future.

It wasn't working that way this time. He'd wrongly accused one of his employees. He'd jumped to conclusions like a teenager instead of questioning her first to make sure his suspicions were correct.

What was there about this young woman that had him in such a state?

Why was it that every time they got together he either yelled at her or made a pass? He shifted uncomfortably. Actually it hadn't really been a pass that had happened between them last Monday afternoon, but she could easily have thought it was.

He'd finally calmed down after that incident and decided it was just one of those innocent encounters that can happen between a man and a woman, until he'd looked up last night and seen Kirsten on the dance floor. He winced as the memory of the shock and pain he'd felt rocked through him once more.

It hadn't even occurred to him that she might have a legitimate reason for being at the banquet. The fact that she and Dane Anderson had the same last name had escaped him completely. His only thought was that he was being set up by a beautiful young woman who wanted something from him and would use any means to get it.

Why had he overreacted so quickly? Was it because it was much more important than it should have been that Kirsten Anderson like him for himself and not because of what he could do for her?

He muttered a curse and dropped his head in his hands.

On Monday morning Kirsten entered her office with apprehension. Over the weekend she'd had time to think about the episode two nights before, and although Courtney Forrester certainly deserved what he'd gotten, her own behavior hadn't exactly been exemplary.

After all, he was her employer. Even though he'd been way off base she should have given him a chance to apologize.

Kirsten sighed and settled down at her desk to begin work when the phone rang. It was Marguerite. "Mr. Forrester sent word down through channels that he wants to see you in his office at twelve o'clock noon," she said crisply. "I assume you'll be free at that time?"

Kirsten's heart sank. She recognized a summons when she heard one. "Yes. Thank you, Marguerite. I'll be there."

Now what? In the four years she'd worked for Evergreen Industries she'd never before been called to the CEO's office. Coming so quickly after the fiasco Saturday night, it didn't bode well for her. Still, he was the one in the wrong, not her.

That thought brought little comfort. It could be argued that the owner of the business is never in the wrong. He could find any number of technical reasons to fire her without even mentioning the real incident.

She somehow got through the morning, and on her way to his office she stopped in the rest room to freshen up. Kirsten saw the dismay that lurked in her eyes as she looked in the mirror to touch up her lipstick and hair. There wasn't much she could do about that, but she was glad she'd worn her gray glen-plaid suit with the pleated skirt and long boxy jacket. It was feminine but strictly business, and even Court couldn't accuse her of trying to seduce him when she wore it.

She presented herself in Court's outer office exactly at noon and found it empty. Tanya's desk was cleared and the chair behind it pushed in. She'd obviously left for lunch.

For a moment Kirsten stood there confused, then decided she'd have to announce herself. Her mouth was dry and her knees felt weak. Had he sent Tanya away because he was angry and didn't want his receptionist to overhear the scene he intended to make?

For a moment she was tempted to turn and run, but she took a deep breath and forced herself to walk across the room. Her knock was answered almost immediately by Courtney Forrester himself. There was no welcoming smile when he opened the door, but the look on his face was one of anxiety rather than anger.

"Hello, Kirsten," he said as he stood aside for her to enter. "It was gracious of you to come."

She was thoroughly rattled. Gracious? She hadn't realized she had a choice.

Before she could think of anything to say he led her toward the lounge area of the large wood-paneled room. It contained a sofa and two upholstered chairs, plus several occasional tables.

"Please, sit down," he said when they got to the sofa, then seated himself beside her.

She had trouble looking away from him. He was dressed in the usual dark business suit, but gone was the arrogant demeanor. He looked almost as uncomfortable as she felt.

Was he trying to soften the blow of a dismissal? After all, he was her father's business acquaintance. He probably wanted to preserve that relationship, if possible, while still getting rid of a troublesome employee.

She felt drops of perspiration sliding down the valley between her breasts. Kirsten very much wanted to keep this job. She'd been happy here, and the thought of being forced to leave made her feel sick.

"Kirsten, I admit I pulled rank in order to see you," Court finally said. "I was afraid you'd refuse if I called direct and asked you to meet me somewhere."

She blinked and her hands tightened into fists in her lap. "Please, Mr. Forrester," she blurted. "If you're going to fire me, just say so. I can't stand the suspense any longer." Her tone was a cross between a plea and a cry for mercy.

Court's eyes widened and his mouth opened, but for a moment no words came. "Fire you!" He finally found his voice. "Whatever gave you that idea?"

Now it was Kirsten who was shocked. "But what was I supposed to think when you summoned me to your office like you did?"

"Good Lord," he muttered, and took one of her trembling hands in his. "I just wanted to apologize for my miserable performance the other night. You wouldn't listen to me then, so I had no choice but to call you into the office this morning and try again."

She'd worked herself into such a state that she could hardly believe what he was saying. "You...you mean you're not going to let me go?"

"Let you go?" His voice had lowered to a gentle murmur. "Kirsten, my biggest problem right now seems to be that I couldn't bring myself to let you go even if I wanted to."

He gently unclenched her fingers and cradled her hand in his. "I don't know what got into me Saturday night. I can only plead insanity, but when I saw you there dancing with one man after the other and all the while flirting with me—"

Kirsten stiffened and sat up straight. "*Flirting* with you!"

Court clasped her hand harder. "No! Don't misunderstand me. I *thought* you were flirting with me. I know now that you were only being friendly, while I was behaving like an idiot."

He seemed so upset that she had no choice but to believe him. Still, he had some more explaining to do before she could be comfortable accepting his apology.

"Why would you think I'd resort to such tactics?" She felt hurt and angry all over again.

He closed his eyes briefly. "I've asked myself that a hundred times in the past thirty-six hours, and I've come up with two reasons. Poor ones, I admit, but then I haven't been thinking exactly straight where you're concerned."

Kirsten's heart fluttered. What did he mean by those last words? Was he trying to tell her that he had special feelings for her?

She pushed that thought away and admonished herself to stop dreaming.

"My first reason is that I've learned over the years to be a little wary of everybody until they've proven that they can be trusted," he said.

She tensed. "And after four years I haven't proved that to your satisfaction yet?" There was outrage in her tone.

He squeezed the hand he held, as though afraid she'd pull it away. With the fingers of the other hand he gently touched her mouth. "Hush," he said anxiously. "Let me finish. About a year after my wife died I met a woman who seemed warm and sympathetic. My marriage had been a happy one, and added to the grief of losing Barbara was the crushing loneliness. I wasn't interested in remarriage, but I badly needed what I thought she was offering—companionship and physical closeness."

Kirsten had to fight the desire to kiss Court's fingers, which were still pressed to her lips and outlining them with little caressing movements. "I later found out she was using our friendship to make business and social contacts with people she could never have approached on her own.''

Kirsten heard the pain of betrayal in his voice even after all this time. With the hand he wasn't holding she reached up and cupped his cheek. He turned his head slightly and kissed her palm.

Her heart pounded and her breathing was ragged as she forgot everything but the man sitting so close beside her. There was a hunger in his eyes, and she knew he was seeing an answering hunger in hers.

"Kirsten," he whispered huskily, and his fingers exerted just enough pressure on her lower lip to part it while his face moved closer to hers.

He was going to kiss her, and she'd never in her life wanted to be kissed so badly!

It was then that the magic spell was broken by a loud knock on the door.

The intruder was a catering-service waiter with lunch. Kirsten wondered if he found it strange that the gentleman who opened the door snapped at him, and the woman on the sofa looked dazed and disappointed. Within minutes he'd set the coffee table with linen mats, china, crystal and silver. After uncovering the bowls of food, he gathered up his containers and left.

Court spoke to her for the first time since the interruption as he walked toward the bar in the corner. "What would you like to drink? I have coffee and almost any liquor or soda."

Kirsten was still shaking. "Coffee, please. Black." Her voice sounded wobbly, and she cleared her throat. "I'm impressed," she said as she eyed the beautifully appointed low table. There was even a small floral centerpiece with lighted candles. "My experience with catered lunches in the office is limited to sending out to McDonald's for hamburgers and fries."

Court laughed, and she noticed that he'd regained his composure, although she was still struggling with hers. "I didn't want you to miss a meal and go hungry all afternoon."

It was an elegant lunch. Crepes stuffed with lobster and covered with béarnaise sauce, spinach salad with black turtle beans and balsamic dressing, and for dessert, fat sweet strawberries dipped in white chocolate.

By the time they'd finished eating they were both relaxed and chatting happily. Court seemed genuinely interested in her background, and she told him about the joys and hazards of growing up in a large, loving family.

"We sort of all grew up together," she concluded. "I was born two weeks after Mom got her B.A. and Dad his M.A. from Stanford. Ingrid came along two years later, and a year after that Mother entered law school. By the time she got her law degree she was pregnant again, and Ruth Anne was born later that summer." Kirsten laughed. "Poor Ruthie. I doubt if she ever learned for sure which of us was the authority figure. We all alternately spoiled her and bossed her around. Still do, for that matter."

Court, who was sitting next to her, grinned. "Sounds to me like 'poor Ruthie' was a very lucky child to be so well loved. Tell me, how old was she when your mother joined the law firm?"

Kirsten thought for a moment. "Mom went to work shortly after Ruth Anne began to walk. We had a live-in babysitter who had been with us since Mom started law school. A woman named Stella Garbeau who was practically part of the family, so there was no problem leaving the baby in her care."

"So you grew up in a family where both parents worked," Court said.

She nodded. "Yes. For as far back as I can remember Mom was either going to school or working."

He frowned. "Didn't you and your sisters feel neglected? Lonely? Didn't you miss not having her there when you got home from school?"

"No, never," Kirsten said vehemently. "There was no need for her to be there; Stella always was. We never came home to an empty house. As for feeling neglected, well, that's silly. We got more attention from our parents than most of our friends got from theirs. When we needed them they were there for us, both of them, even if they had to leave work in the middle of the day."

She turned to face Court, eager to make him understand. "It's not the quantity of time that parents spend with their children that's important, Mr. Forrester. It's the quality. Dad and Mom gave us all their attention when they were with us."

Court's expressive brown eyes watched her mouth as she spoke. "Please, call me Court," he said softly.

"Court," she whispered, sampling the name as their gazes melded. "Is that proper?"

"Probably not," he murmured. "But it's way past time for us to be on a first-name basis."

"Court," she said, trying to keep the conversation on track in spite of her wildly fluctuating pulse. "What was the other reason you thought I was trying to use you?"

He blinked. "Use me?"

Kirsten smiled, delighted that his thoughts were apparently as muddled as hers were.

"You said there were two reasons why you thought I was trying to establish a . . . a relationship . . . to get you to agree to the child-care center."

The bemused expression on his face disappeared. "Oh, that. It's not important. I was obviously wrong."

A twinge of apprehension tugged at the back of her mind. "But you said—"

"I'm sorry I mentioned it," he hedged. "It was just a fleeting thought."

She frowned. "It couldn't have been very fleeting if it bothered you enough to convince you I'd do something unprofessional."

Kirsten wished that she'd never brought up the subject, but now that she had it was important to her to know the answer.

He restlessly shifted position and made a dismissing gesture with his hands. "Kirsten, I've apologized and admitted I was an idiot to ever have distrusted you. Now let's drop it."

The twinge of apprehension had grown to full-blown foreboding. "I'm sorry, but the fact that you're reluctant to discuss it makes me certain I have the right to know."

Court stood and began pacing, a nervous habit she recognized from the last time they'd quarreled in his office. "I disagree," he said, and she heard the anxiety in his tone, "but since you feel so strongly about it I'll tell you. Just please remember that it was an unworthy thought, and I'm ashamed that it ever crossed my mind."

He stopped pacing and turned to face her. "I was so insanely upset and talked to you the way I did because I was afraid that you had . . . had come on to me here in the office last Monday only because you wanted to soften me up for—"

Kirsten felt the blood drain from her face, and leaped out of her chair, seething with embarrassment and fury. "*I* came on to *you*?" she shouted. "Is that how you saw it?"

"No!" Court reached for her but she whirled away from him. "Dammit, I knew this was going to happen. I'm an engineer, not a poet. I don't know the words to express—"

"Oh, you were doing just fine," she snapped. "I get the picture. You were here thinking nothing but pure thoughts, and I came in and tried to seduce you so that you'd arrange to have other people's children taken care of."

This time he caught her and held her by the upper arms. "That's not what I meant," he said. "If I was having pure thoughts about you before you came here that day, it was the last time. Since holding you in my arms I haven't been able to think of anything but how to get you back in them. It's not your fault, it's mine. You were so sweet, and warm, and eager to comfort..."

She jerked herself out of his grasp. "Well, pardon me." Kirsten knew she was out of control, but she couldn't seem to help it. It was humiliating to know that he thought she'd initiated that impromptu embrace. "I absolutely guarantee you that it won't happen again. Now, if you'll excuse me, I'm late for an appointment."

She rushed out the door and let it slam behind her.

On Wednesday morning Court arrived at the office long before anyone else was around. His reasoning was that he couldn't sleep anyway, so he might as well get some work done. The problem was that he couldn't concentrate on his work, either.

After reading a paragraph of the quarterly financial report for the third time and still not knowing what it said, he threw it down on his desk and swore. What in hell was the matter with him? Why was he letting a girl who was young enough to be his daughter upset him so badly?

Maybe he was having a mid-life crisis. He sure wasn't getting any younger. His forty-fourth birthday was coming up in a couple of months, but growing older had never bothered him before. Actually, since he'd still been in his twenties when his small computer had started him on the road to success beyond his wildest hopes, he'd always welcomed each added year of maturity as an asset.

It must be the loneliness. He'd thought that after three years he had that under control, but who knows what the melancholy isolation of grief can do to the subconscious? Maybe he just needed to get away, take a vacation, possibly even invite a companion along. If the problem was his neglected libido then it was time to do something about it. He knew several sophisticated women who would be happy to travel with him for a few weeks without expecting a long-term commitment.

He stood and walked over to the window. Cars were streaming into the parking lot below. Soon the building would be filled with busy people.

He looked at his watch. It was seven-thirty. At ten o'clock he had a meeting scheduled with Kirsten and her committee. He needed to talk to her and straighten out the misunderstanding his ineptness with words had caused, but he'd do that later when they could be alone.

Afterward he was going to call his travel agent and arrange to leave as soon as possible. It didn't matter where he went. All he wanted was to get the hell away from the sweet, compassionate lady who was tying him in knots.

At five minutes past ten, Court strolled into the small conference room next to his office and was greeted by three women and a man. There was also a stenographer to take notes, but no sign of Kirsten.

Court frowned. "Did Ms. Anderson say how late she expected to be?" he asked the group in general.

It was Sandra Taylor who answered. "She isn't coming. She asked me to head the committee for this meeting."

Court felt a sense of disappointment like a blow to the stomach. Then anxiety crept in. "Is she ill?"

"No, sir. I believe something unexpected came up. She won't be able to join us."

The anxiety disappeared, replaced by regret. She was avoiding him. She had no intention of meeting with him again. He muttered a short "Excuse me for a few minutes," and strode out of the room.

Kirsten was sitting at her desk, anxiously wondering what was going on in the meeting upstairs when the door opened and Court came in. She stared in surprise as he shut it and walked over to where she was sitting. There was an unreadable look on his face as he reached out his hands to her.

Without thinking she put her hands in his and he pulled her up and into his arms. The action was so unexpected that she raised her head to question him and saw the glittering determination in his eyes just before his mouth covered hers.

An involuntary gasp parted her lips and his tongue invaded the moist freshness in an intimacy that both startled and inflamed her. *Dear God, I must be dreaming,* she thought as she leaned against him and clasped her arms around his neck.

He pulled her closer still until she could feel the muscle and sinew of his hard, warm body beneath the fine wool of the blue suit he wore. His kiss was even more exciting than she'd dreamed it would be, and she gave herself up to the wonder of it. She allowed her tongue to stroke his, and he moaned softly as he returned the caress.

He broke off the exploration of her mouth slowly and brushed his lips down her throat to a wildly sensitive spot just beneath her ear. A purring sound escaped her as her arms tightened to hold him more firmly.

"Now do you understand how I feel about you?" he asked huskily as he caught the lobe of her ear gently between his teeth. "I've wanted to do this ever since you walked into my office the first time and I realized you weren't a teenager."

She stroked the bare flesh of his nape. "Why didn't you then, instead of apologizing when you did hold me?"

He raised his head and looked at her. "Sweetheart, you can't mean that. I'm almost as old as your father. I don't expect anything from you. I'm certainly not going to take advantage of you, but I had to let you know how it is with me because you kept misunderstanding my awkward attempts to conceal it."

Kirsten tried to protest, but he kissed her once more, quickly, tenderly, and released her. "I came down here to get you. I want you upstairs. You started this investigation into the advisability of setting up a day-care center, and I expect you to finish it."

Kirsten blinked. "I—I assumed . . ."

"That's the trouble," he said gently. "You do too much assuming. If you'd ask me what I want or how I feel once in a while instead of assuming that you know, we'd get along a lot better. Now gather up whatever you need to present your case and come along. We're already keeping five people waiting who have plenty of other things to do."

He was right. She'd assumed that Court would be relieved that she'd turned the meeting over to someone else, but happily she'd been wrong. She didn't dare give in to her joy at finding out just how wrong or she'd never have been able to keep her mind on the business at hand.

She retrieved her folder from the drawer, and he took her arm as they left the office.

The members of the committee were seated at the conference table when Kirsten and Court arrived. He smiled at them. "Ms. Anderson found that she was able to join us after all," he said, and seated her in the chair beside his.

Court started off by asking Kirsten to go over the proposal again for the benefit of all of them.

"Certainly, Mr. Forrester," she said, and hoped no one noticed the tremor in her voice.

For nearly two hours they explored the suggestions point by point. Court asked questions of the other committee members, who were supervisors in various departments of the company. Sandra Taylor told her about her experience with Annie.

"Annie was one of my assembly-line workers," Sandra began. "She'd quit school in the tenth grade to get married, and had four children before her husband ran out on her. She was ambitious and skilled with her hands. Her mother took care of her kids so she could work, and she was proud of being self-supporting. Then her mother got sick and couldn't care for the kids anymore. Annie couldn't afford to pay to have all four of them taken care of, so she was forced to give up her job and go on welfare. Everybody lost. Annie gave up her independence, we lost a trained employee and the taxpayers have another family to support."

Ruby Freeman broke in. "It's not only the mothers who need babysitters. There was a young man in my department who showed so much promise that Evergreen Industries arranged for him to go to college while working for us. He got his degree and was fast becoming one of our most brilliant engineers when his wife was killed and he was left with a six-month-old son. The few child-care centers that take infants all had long waiting lists. He finally resigned and went back East to work for a firm that had on-site care for their employees' small children. We not only lost a valued employee, but all the money we'd invested in his education."

Court listened attentively. There were other stories from Lucy Vaughan and Robert Bradford before Court finally brought the meeting to a close. "It's lunchtime, and we've done about all we can for today. I'll get back to you after I've had time to look into the matter further and do some research of my own."

He stood, signaling dismissal. "Thank you for bringing this to my attention. I have to admit that I'm still not convinced that Evergreen Industries should get into the child-care business, but I'm willing to consider it."

He turned to face Kirsten. "Kirsten, stay a few minutes, please. I have some things to go over with you."

She stood with the rest of them and walked away from him to the other side of the room. The door shut behind the departing committee, and Court's voice was low and gentle when he spoke from behind her. "Are you still mad at me?"

No, Kirsten thought, not angry. How could she possibly be angry with him after he'd kissed her with so much passion? But there was still a lingering hurt and embarrassment that her offer of friendship, of caring, could have been so misinterpreted.

Kirsten was a toucher. Her whole family was. It was the way she'd been raised. Her first instinct when sharing someone's joy or grief or good fortune was to touch. Usually to hug.

Her intent had never been misunderstood before. Not even by the men she'd dated. She wasn't a tease, and no one had ever accused her of being one. No one but her boss, the owner of the company.

"No, Court, I'm not mad at you," she said, and there was a catch in her voice. "I'm just embarrassed that you mistook my compassion for... for flirting."

She felt the pressure of his footsteps as he moved toward her across the thick carpeting. "Oh, honey, I didn't. The thought never even occurred to me until I saw you at the country club and lost my reason altogether."

He cupped her shoulders with his hands. "Do you want me to admit that I was jealous of all those men you were dancing with? I was, you know. Part of me ached to hold you in my arms and move with you to the rhythm of the music, even while the demon inside was insisting that you were trying to con me."

She gave in to the need to lean back against the long length of his firm body, and he put his arms around her waist and rubbed his cheek in her hair. "I'm glad you care enough about me to be jealous," she admitted, and put her hands over his where they crossed on her flat stomach.

He pulled her closer so that her hips and thighs were cradled against his. "You're sweet to want to make me feel better, but it's not necessary. I know how impossible this situation is. I wouldn't have told you if it hadn't been necessary to help you understand why I sometimes behave like an idiot."

What he was doing and what he was saying were totally at odds. She prayed that his need to act was more compelling than his convictions as she tipped her head back against his shoulder, making the long line of her throat available to his mouth. "I don't understand why you're so determined to deny that you're attracted to me. Surely you've noticed that my response has been anything but cool."

She shivered as he trailed small, nibbling kisses down her exposed throat, sending tiny shocks through her body to her feminine core.

"I'm not denying my feelings," he said huskily. "I'm just trying to keep them under control."

He released her and stepped away. She had to clench her fists to keep herself from reaching for him and imploring him to continue to hold her.

"I'm an authority figure to you, Kirsten, on two counts," he said, and this time his voice was ragged. "I'm not only your employer, but I'm a generation older than you. Either of those things would be enough to intimidate a girl as young as you, and I'm not going to take advantage of it."

He'd struck a nerve and she bristled. "I'm not a girl, I'm a woman, and I make my own decisions. If these things don't bother me why should they upset you?"

He turned from her and ran his fingers through his hair. "Because no matter what you call yourself, you're still very young. You don't need a man my age taking up your time. You'll want to marry and have children."

For the first time Kirsten felt the chill of foreboding. "You don't intend to marry again?"

Court hesitated. "I don't rule out the possibility. I was married for a long time, and living alone is lonely. In spite of what you've read in the papers and magazines, I'm not a middle-aged Casanova. In the past couple of years I've dated a few women, but they were mature and sophisticated. They didn't expect anything from me but a good time. If I marry again it will be for companionship. I've been in love, and once was enough."

Chapter Four

Kirsten didn't see or hear from Court again for the rest of the week. Their parting on Wednesday had been awkward at the very least. After his assertion that even though he was strongly attracted to her he had no intention of pursuing a relationship, there was nothing else to say. They'd left the conference room and gone their separate ways.

That wasn't what Kirsten wanted. Her feelings for Court were too strong to be infatuation. He was an exciting man, handsome and sexy, but with a depth of maturity that set him apart from the younger men she'd dated. She knew she could easily fall in love with him. He filled her thoughts and haunted her dreams, and left her wretched and edgy. Every time her office door opened or the phone rang she jumped, hoping it was he, but it never was.

On Saturday she did the laundry and shopped for groceries as usual, then went to an antique show with a friend who was a collector. Later that evening she attended a movie with one of the men she'd been dating.

Kirsten went to church with her parents and Ruth Anne on Sunday morning, and afterward had lunch with them. In the afternoon she was escorted to a cocktail party by one of the men she'd grown up with.

As usual it was a busy weekend with family and friends, but as Kirsten got ready for bed that night, she had the restless sensation that she was just marking time, that there was a lot more to life that she was missing out on. She was well aware that she'd never had this feeling until she'd been held and kissed by Courtney Forrester.

When Kirsten woke on Monday morning it was raining. Certainly not unusual for the first week of November in northern California, but the dreary dimness of her rooms left her vaguely depressed.

By the time she got to her office she felt chilled and damp even though she was wearing her unisex dress-for-success dark raincoat. She hated it and sometimes wondered if her career really would disintegrate if she showed up for work in a shiny bright red coat with a hat to match. How much longer were she and her sister business women going to be such sheep that they let men tell them how to dress?

She was feeling thoroughly rebellious and out of sorts a short time later when the telephone rang. "Kirsten Anderson speaking," she answered, and realized that she sounded as grumpy as she felt.

"Kirsten, this is Court," said the baritone voice on the other end, sending sunbeams into the dark corners of her depression. "I know this is short notice, but could you clear your calendar for tomorrow and go with me to visit a few day-care centers?"

She wanted to tell him she'd go with him anywhere, anytime, but she knew he didn't want to hear that. It didn't bode well for her peace of mind that she was more excited about seeing him again than she was about his escalated interest in child-care centers!

Kirsten struggled to get her errant feelings under control. "I'm sure I can," she said in her best professional manner. "Will you hold for a minute while I check?"

She flipped the page of her appointment calendar. "There's nothing here that I can't reschedule," she told him. "Do you know which centers you'd like to visit, or do you want me to make some appointments for you?"

"My secretary's already taken care of it. We'll be concentrating on the downtown area. You'd better clear Wednesday, too, because I have a lead on a company that's in the process of setting up an on-site center, but we haven't been able to contact them yet." He hesitated. "Will that be inconvenient?"

Kirsten actually shook her head in her eagerness to reassure him. "No, not at all. I'm delighted that you're taking so much interest."

"I told you I would," he said softly, more like a lover than a boss. "I'll pick you up tomorrow morning at your office about nine-thirty."

The following morning Kirsten was up at five o'clock. She chided herself for acting like a star-struck schoolgirl all the time she was carefully applying makeup and rejecting one outfit after another in an effort to look her very best. Should she wear a suit? Maybe a dress? How about slacks, since she wouldn't be in the office?

She finally settled on a midcalf length, camel-colored suede skirt and a rust turtleneck sweater with matching wraparound shawl. To this she added a wide belt and high boots. Definitely not the type of thing she'd wear to work!

When Court arrived at her tiny office to pick her up, he was dressed as usual in a business suit, but his brown eyes lit with admiration as his gaze roamed over her. "You look very beautiful," he said, then grinned. "If I were fifteen years younger I'd whistle."

Kirsten glowed with delight. "You can whistle at me if I can whistle at you," she said.

"Deal," he replied, and puckered up.

They each emitted the traditional wolf whistle, in unison, then howled with laughter.

"We'd better get out of here," Court said, still chuckling, "before we have to explain our juvenile behavior to Marguerite. Where's your coat?"

"I didn't wear one," she said as she picked up the oversize shawl that matched her sweater. "Since it's no longer raining and the sun's out I brought this instead."

She swirled it around her shoulders and picked up her purse. Court offered her his arm, and she hesitated. "What's the matter, Kirsten?" he asked. "Don't you want me to escort you through the building?"

He looked hurt, and she couldn't let him think the wrong thing. "I'd like that very much," she answered truthfully. "But do you think it's proper?"

His gaze penetrated hers. "I own the company. I can do anything I want to, but if you feel it would compromise you . . ."

Still holding his gaze, she put her hand at the crook of his arm and he hugged it close to his side. "I'm ready if you are," she said, and wondered just what she was getting herself into. Whatever it was, it was worth it to walk so close beside him with her hand nestled between his arm and his ribs.

The first day-care center they visited was in an old Victorian home. The ground floor had been remodeled to accommodate the children, and there were two attendants. The manager, a woman in her late thirties or early forties, was expecting them. She was happily cooperative, answering their questions, showing them the modifications she'd made to conform to health and safety laws, and even going over her fee schedule.

When they left Court was beaming. "If that's a sample of the care available to the children of working parents in the area, then I don't see any reason to duplicate it in our building," he told Kirsten as he maneuvered his black Lincoln Town Car into the stream of traffic. "Those kids were getting excellent supervision."

Kirsten had been sure he was going to say something like that, and she was prepared. "That's true, they were," she agreed. "But did you notice that none of the children were under three years old?"

Court turned to look at her as they stopped for a red light. "No, I didn't."

"I did, and I asked her about it while the other attendant was showing you around. She said they don't accept infants, and toddlers have to be potty-trained before they'll take them."

He drove off again as the light turned green. "She's got all the children her license will allow; apparently she doesn't have to take infants."

"That's exactly what I'm getting at," Kirsten said. "She has a waiting list of parents anxious to get their children in, so she doesn't have to bother with infants and young toddlers who need so much more care. You're looking at this like a businessman, not a parent."

"That's not so surprising," Court replied, "since I *am* a businessman. I still feel that women who have infants should stay home and take care of them."

If Kirsten had had something in her hand she'd have thrown it at him. "Dammit, Court, take off your blinders and look around you. Most women are not in a position to stay home and take care of their babies. Too many of them are heads of their families, and a good share of those never receive support payments from their children's father. Not all mothers work because they want to. For most of them it's a choice between that and going on welfare.''

He pulled over to the curb and parked the car, then turned toward her. ''All right, honey, I'm sorry. I don't mean to sound like a self-righteous prig. It's just that I feel strongly on the subject. Surely you're going to grant me the same right to express my opinion that you've been exercising so energetically.''

Kirsten realized that again she'd overreacted. He was right, his conviction was just as valid as hers. Why did she always get so emotional when she was with him?

''Yes, of course I am, Cou—uh...Mr. Forrester.'' She was confused as to just how friendly he wanted her to be with him.

He put his fingers under her chin and lifted her face so that she had to look at him. ''Court, Kirsten,'' he said huskily. ''It's a simple one-syllable name. Much easier to say than Mr. Forrester.'' His tempting mouth turned up at the corners in a teasing grin. ''Please don't just use it when you're railing at me about something.''

The man was totally devastating when he wanted to be, Kirsten thought as her bones turned to jelly. Every time he touched her she lost her ability to function on anything but a sensuously charged level.

His eyes sparkled and his gaze settled on her lips as she nervously ran her tongue over them. His hand caressed her chin, and she had an almost irresistible urge to touch his finely chiseled face with her fingers.

''Court,'' she whispered, like a child learning a new word.

''That's my girl,'' he murmured just before his mouth covered hers, softly, sweetly, and brought her totally under his spell.

She couldn't keep herself from responding, but she did manage to restrain her arms from stealing around his neck and holding him. She had no idea what he wanted of her.

Kirsten came out of the romantic haze slowly as Court lifted his head, breaking off the kiss gently. He put his forehead against hers and sighed. "I've had a hell of a time staying away from you," he whispered softly. Before she could pull herself together enough to tell him she'd missed him, too, he straightened up and announced, "We'd better go in before we attract a crowd."

She blinked. "Go in? Where...?" She turned her head and looked out the window. They were in a shabby, run-down area with broken sidewalks and houses in need of repair and paint. "Where are we?"

He chuckled. "We're parked in front of the second day-care center on our list," he explained patiently, obviously enjoying her confusion.

She ignored the blush she felt creeping up to her hairline. Their destination was an old one-story house built on a high foundation with at least ten steps leading up to the sagging porch. There was a worn old gate at the top that any active, imaginative small child could figure out how to open. If one of them did and then fell down the stairs, he or she would land on the cement sidewalk and almost certainly be hurt.

"I hope it's in better shape on the inside than it is on the outside," she muttered as she surveyed the chipped and peeling paint. One glass pane in the front window was gone, replaced by a piece of plywood, and the front lawn was mostly overgrown weeds.

As they climbed the rickety steps they could hear the din of children quarreling and crying. There were broken toys tossed around on the porch, and some of them now had points and ragged edges. Kirsten was dismayed and wondered how long it had been since this place had been inspected.

The heavyset woman who answered the door was dressed in faded jeans and an old sweatshirt that had a rip across the arm. Her black hair was tousled, and there was a streak of dirt on her cheek. Court introduced himself and Kirsten, and the woman, a Mrs. Bronson, opened the screen and let them in.

The inside was a disaster. It was reasonably clean but badly cluttered. Not just with the children's things, but with boxes, papers, articles of clothing strewn around and dirty dishes littering the dining-room table and the kitchen. They had to walk carefully to avoid stepping on or stumbling over the toys the children had left lying on the floor.

One small child clung to Mrs. Bronson and cried while two others ran through the house yelling at each other.

Kirsten felt Court tense beside her. "Mrs. Bronson, if we've come at a bad time—"

"No, sir," the woman interrupted. "Just let me quiet these kids down." She turned and shouted in the direction of the noise. "Hey, you two, shut up and stop that runnin' around."

She took off after them, and Court and Kirsten could hear her scolding as she herded them out the back door. Before either adult could overcome their shock and comment, Mrs. Bronson returned carrying the child who had been crying.

"Sorry," she said. "Them two fight all the time. Don't know what I'm gonna do with 'em."

She put the little girl down and started moving rumpled clothes and stuffed toys off the worn sofa. "There, now you can sit down. Sorry the place is such a mess. The kids was all inside yesterday because of the rain, and I haven't had time to straighten it up again."

Kirsten felt sick. The woman was doing the best she was capable of, but they'd still have to report her.

Later, after they'd bid Mrs. Bronson goodbye and left, neither spoke until they'd gotten into the car and were several blocks away from the house. Then Court glanced at

Kirsten. "Are there many care-givers like that one?" he asked in a tight voice.

"I hope not," Kirsten said with a sigh. "At least not licensed ones, but unfortunately the child-welfare department doesn't have enough staff to inspect them as often as they should. At least Mrs. Bronson seems to watch the children carefully, but her sloppy housekeeping and her disregard for safety regulations..." Kirsten shuddered.

She turned in her seat so that her whole attention was focused on Court. "That's a classic example of what I've been trying to get across to you. She's a nice, well-meaning lady with an incomplete education and a low self-image whose husband ran out on her. She's struggling to support herself and her child in the only way she can, babysitting. Unfortunately she doesn't seem to know much about that, either."

Court glanced at Kirsten. "I'm going to have to report her."

Kirsten nodded. "I know. They'll take her license away and she'll have no choice but to go on welfare. Once she does she'll probably never get off it. It wouldn't have to be that way, Court, if businesses would provide child care at a reasonable rate for their employees."

"I don't see what difference that would make. The woman's not trained for any kind of job."

"But Evergreen Industries could train her." Kirsten's voice throbbed with conviction. "There's always a shortage of assembly-line workers. The task is simple and easily learned, but it also starts at a pretty low wage. Mrs. Bronson couldn't afford the going rate for child care and pay her other bills, too, but if we had a day-care center with an escalating charge scale, she could go to work, get some training and Evergreen would benefit as much as she would."

Kirsten had been so caught up in her argument that she'd failed to notice where they were until Court swung the car into a small parking lot. "It's lunchtime," he said in reply to her look of surprise. "You didn't have other plans, did you?"

With a glance she recognized the building at the front of the lot as a well-known downtown restaurant that was a favorite noontime eating place for business people and upscale shoppers.

"No, none," she answered with a smile. "And now that you mention it, I'm starved."

Court had obviously made a reservation because when he gave the hostess his name they were seated ahead of several others who were waiting. When the cocktail waitress arrived, he ordered a martini and she asked for coffee.

"Don't you drink?" he asked as the waitress walked away. "Or do I intimidate you?"

"Neither, but I don't drink in the middle of the day." She chuckled. "I need all my wits about me. Especially when I'm trying to talk my hardheaded boss into doing something he doesn't feel is necessary."

Court affected a grossly offended look, but there was a twinkle in his eye. "Hardheaded? Me? Why, I'm putty in the hands of a bright and beautiful woman. You'll probably have me begging to be allowed to set up a day-care center before you're finished with me."

Kirsten hooted with delight. "Sure you will, but I'm not going to hold my breath until it happens. I—"

She was interrupted by a woman calling to them as she walked toward their table. "Dad, imagine finding you here."

They both jumped with surprise, and Court stood as Kirsten watched two young women making their way across the room. Apparently the blond beauty who was speaking was Court's daughter. The other one had brown hair and wore glasses.

"Noelle, what are you doing here?" Court asked as he hugged the blonde. "Aren't you supposed to be in school?"

She laughed and kissed him. "Our class this afternoon was canceled so Faith and I decided to go shopping. May we sit with you?" she asked, eyeing the two empty chairs at the table. "We don't have reservations and there's a line waiting to get in."

Court hesitated and looked at Kirsten, who sat quietly and gave no indication of whether she agreed or disagreed. She was aware that Court's lovely daughter had been covertly watching her even as they were walking toward the table, and the vibes Kirsten got were not friendly.

Before he could answer, Noelle pulled out a chair and sat down, ignoring Kirsten as she indicated that her friend should do the same. Faith stood with her hand on the back of the chair, seemingly embarrassed, until Court nodded. "Please join us, Faith. How are you?"

Her rather plain face brightened with a sweet smile as she sat down. "I'm fine, thank you, Mr. Forrester."

Court put his hand over Kirsten's as it lay on the table and turned to the two newcomers. "Kirsten, I'd like you to meet my daughter, Noelle, and her roommate, Faith Ross. Ladies, this is Kirsten Anderson."

The three women murmured greetings rather awkwardly, and Kirsten watched Court's daughter as she turned away to chat with him. There was very little resemblance between the two. Noelle was small and fair with golden blond hair that cascaded down her back to her waist. Her eyes were blue and her features were delicate. She had a look of fragility, but Kirsten recognized the core of steel in her personality.

Noelle was dressed in a shapeless, somewhat ragged layered style that looked as if it had been assembled from someone's attic. However, Kirsten recognized the couturier quality and knew it had come from one of the exclusive high-priced funky boutiques that catered to high school and college girls.

Noelle continued to ignore Kirsten as she talked to Court. "Daddy, I'm glad we ran into you. I've found a dress that's exactly what I've been looking for to wear to the home-coming dance, but I need some money."

Court frowned. "Put it on your bank card. That's what you've got it for."

Noelle's bright smile dimmed. "Yeah, well, there's a bit of a problem. I'm over my limit."

Court glared at her. "Over your limit! You can't be. I just paid your last bill less than a month ago."

She looked down at her napkin. "I know, Dad, but I've had a lot of expenses lately. Sorority assessments, and new tires for my BMW, and . . ." she shrugged ". . . you know."

He sighed. "Then buy the dress out of your allowance."

Noelle blinked. "I—I don't have enough of my allowance left," she said in a small voice.

Kirsten was acutely uncomfortable at witnessing this scene between father and daughter, which should have been con-ducted in private. She glanced at Faith and saw that Noelle's friend looked equally ill at ease. Leaning closer, she mur-mured, "I suggest we take a trip to the ladies' room."

Faith nodded eagerly, and they both stood. "Excuse us," Kirsten murmured and started to walk away, but Court grabbed her hand.

"Where are you going?" he asked anxiously, and she could tell from his look and tone that he thought she was leaving the restaurant.

She devoutly wished she could, but it would cause a scene and that was the last thing she wanted. "We'll be right back," she said. "We're just going to the powder room." ·

"Oh." He looked relieved and let go of her hand.

When the door to the ladies' lounge swung shut behind them, Faith breathed a sigh. "Darn, I wish Noelle wouldn't pick the times I'm with her to hit her Dad up for money."

"Does she do this often?" Kirsten asked, knowing she shouldn't pry, but too interested not to.

"Yeah, quite a bit. Oh, don't get me wrong, I like Noelle. She's a lot of fun, but spoiled rotten. All she has to do is turn on the tears, or the charm, whichever suits the occasion, and Mr. Forrester will cave in every time. He's a really great guy, and I hate to see her take advantage of him that way."

"I imagine he's trying to be both father and mother to his children and overdoes it sometimes."

Faith shrugged. "I suppose," she said, and walked over to the large mirror. "Are you a college student, too?" she asked Kirsten's image beside her in the glass.

Kirsten smiled. "No, I graduated from U.C. Santa Cruz four years ago. I work for Mr. Forrester at Evergreen."

Faith smiled back. "Lucky you. I'll bet he's a neat boss."

"Yes, he is," Kirsten agreed, and wondered again where her unorthodox relationship with her "neat boss" was heading.

After whiling away fifteen minutes in the lounge, Kirsten and Faith returned to their table. Court stood and looked at them with a puzzled expression. "I was just about to send Noelle to see if anything was wrong."

The two women took their seats. "Everything's fine," Kirsten said. "We were just getting acquainted. Sorry if we held you up."

Noelle was all smiles as she turned to her friend. "We can go back to Dominique's and pick up the dress," she said happily. "Dad agrees that I really need it."

"That's not what I—" Whatever Court was going to say was interrupted by the waiter who came to take their order.

Kirsten recognized Dominique's as an exclusive French import boutique, and knew that his daughter's dress had cost Court a bundle. She felt a twinge of disappointment that he had allowed Noelle to twist him around her finger so easily, though at the same time she knew it was none of her business how he chose to raise his children.

On the other hand, this "child" was a senior in college and should have been developing a sense of responsibility for herself.

After they'd consulted the menu and placed their orders, Noelle focused her attention on Kirsten for the first time. "I understand you're one of Dad's employees, Ms. Anderson," she said. "Are you a typist or something?"

"Noelle!" Court admonished, but Kirsten spoke before he could continue.

"Or something," she confirmed, with just the right touch of dignity. Noelle's lack of manners was degrading only to herself, but Kirsten was stung by Court's apparent haste in explaining to his daughter that his companion was just an employee.

"Ms. Anderson is assistant manager of the personnel department," Court said with a mixture of embarrassment and anger. "We've been visiting day-care centers this morning."

Noelle's eyes widened. "Whatever for? Can't Ms. Anderson find her own babysitter?"

Kirsten had grown up with the children of the well-to-do and she'd known several spoiled rich brats over the years. She had no intention of rising to Noelle's bait. Instead she sat quietly and waited for Court to handle it.

He did. "Now look here, young lady," he said, and his tone was low and authoritative. "I've had enough of your rudeness. Either settle down and mind your manners or find another table."

Noelle looked truly shocked. "I—I'm sorry," she apologized in a voice that trembled slightly. "I didn't mean to be rude. I was just trying to get to know Ms. Anderson better."

Noelle sounded truly surprised that anyone would think she'd been rude, and Kirsten was quite sure that she was the only one at the table who recognized the insincerity of Court's daughter's apology. Kirsten had seen the fury in Noelle's eyes before Noelle could disguise it and knew that she'd just pounded another nail in the coffin of any hopes she may have had for a relationship with Court.

She'd made an enemy of his beloved daughter.

During the meal Noelle quickly ingratiated herself back into her father's favor and dominated the conversation, and Court. She kept up a running monologue on her activities, both social and scholastic. Kirsten learned that she was into everything: the homecoming committee, the school newspaper, the drama department's upcoming play and numerous sorority affairs.

At intervals Court tried to include Kirsten and Faith, but Faith was taking her cue from Kirsten. Neither of them would play the game. They answered questions put to them, but refused to try to take the spotlight away from Noelle.

Finally the interminable luncheon was over. Noelle embraced her father and thanked him profusely for the money he'd given her. She even remembered to say a brief goodbye to Kirsten before hurrying Faith out of the restaurant on their way back to buy the dress she coveted.

It wasn't until Kirsten and Court returned to the car that an uneasy silence settled around them as each sought a way to avoid the subject of the encounter with Noelle.

They'd driven several miles without speaking before Kirsten realized they were approaching an especially green and luxuriant area on the outskirts of the city.

She peered out the window at the huge old walnut and elm trees that lined the paved road. "Where are we going?" she finally asked.

"I'm taking you to my house, where we can talk," Court answered.

"To your house?" Her voice sounded as if it had risen an octave, and she cleared her throat.

"It's just a little way farther, and it's the only place we can be alone where no one will interrupt."

A few minutes later he turned onto a narrow private road and began to climb the hilly landscape. After about a mile they came to a high brick wall and followed it to a wide pair of wrought-iron gates. Court swung into the driveway and stopped at the small guardhouse where a uniformed man greeted him and pushed a button that opened the gates. Court drove on through and up the curving road. Ahead of them at the top of the hill was a rambling, ultramodern house built of wood and glass set in a grove of shade trees. It was surrounded by green, beautifully manicured lawns and brilliantly colored flower gardens.

Kirsten's heart nearly stopped beating. Was this multi-million dollar estate where Court lived? Obviously it was, but why was she so surprised? She'd known Courtney Forrester was one of the richest men in the country. Still, she'd never imagined him in a home like this, and the reality was unsettling.

He stopped the car in front of the house, and immediately a man appeared to open the door for him. "Don't bother to put the car away, George," he said as he stepped out. "We'll be using it again."

There was another tall wrought-iron gate across the heavy front door, and Court rang the bell. Kirsten watched, both fascinated and appalled, as the door was opened by a tall, raw-boned, middle-aged woman. She had short black hair and wore a plain black dress, black oxfords and a dour expression.

"Good afternoon, Mr. Forrester," she said, and pushed a button on the wall that released the gate.

Court swung it open and motioned for Kirsten to precede him as he nodded to the woman. "Thank you, Mrs.

Underhill," he answered. "We won't need anything else." The woman disappeared into another part of the house.

Kirsten looked around her. The entryway was two stories high with gleaming hardwood floors and an imposing staircase that curved up the wall to their right. On either side of the door were wide glass panels that rose to the roof. From the outside they'd looked black, but on the inside they were clear and provided a panoramic view of the tree-lined driveway and the front lawns and gardens.

Court took her into an enormous formal living room with an exotic onyx fireplace and several furniture groupings in shades of blue and gray. The front and southside walls were glass, and the view from them was stunning. The house sat in the middle of an acreage that could have easily outclassed most parks.

"Oh, Court, this place is magnificent," she said.

He seemed preoccupied and didn't stop but continued on through the room. "Thank you, but I didn't bring you here to show off the house."

He ushered her through a doorway into a smaller but equally luxurious sitting room, where the south wall was also glass, and the fireplace from the other room went through to a backup one that was black onyx, as well.

"Would you like something to drink?" he asked as he seated her on the gray velvet sofa.

"No, thank you, but don't let me stop you from having one."

He grimaced and sat down beside her. "I think not. Now I'm the one who has to keep my wits about me. Kirsten, I'm sorry our luncheon was interrupted, and I apologize for my daughter's behavior. I've never known her to act so badly."

Kirsten suspected that he'd just never been so aware of her impudence before this. "I think she was upset because you were with me."

He looked startled. "But she doesn't even know you."

"True, but she doesn't have to know me to feel threatened by me."

"Threatened by you?" His tone was incredulous. "That's nonsense. Why would Noelle feel threatened by you?" He took her hand and raised it to his lips. "You're the gentlest, most compassionate person I've ever known."

He kissed the back of her hand, then turned it over and ran the tip of his tongue over her palm, sending shivers down her back.

Kirsten fought against her desire to move into his arms and ignore the warning signals that were flashing in her brain, but her strong sense of self-preservation won out.

For a smart man, Court was surprisingly blind where his daughter was concerned. He hadn't yet realized that he'd been presented with an obstacle to his feelings for Kirsten that made the age difference and the employer-employee problem insignificant by comparison.

Noelle Forrester would move heaven and hell to prevent her father from becoming involved with the likes of Kirsten Anderson!

Chapter Five

Carefully, so as not to appear to be rejecting Court's caress, Kirsten pulled her hand away and clasped it with the one in her lap. "You and Noelle seem very close," she said without looking at him.

"We are." He didn't hesitate to confirm it. "My children were the only thing that saved my sanity when my wife died, and I tried to fill the void that was left by their mother's passing."

"I'm sure Noelle was a special comfort. Sort of taking over some of the duties of the woman of the household." Kirsten was being very cautious. She didn't want him to think she was prying into his private life.

"Noelle had just turned eighteen at the time," he said impatiently. "She was a child, not a woman."

Kirsten smiled. He sounded like her mother when she talked about Ruth Anne. "You're wrong, Court. An eighteen-year-old female is very much a woman. Immature to be sure, but a woman all the same. Was Noelle in college?"

"No, she'd just graduated from high school, but she'd been accepted at Vassar for the fall term."

Kirsten was brought up short. "Oh. I thought she'd always attended San Jose State."

"She has," Court assured her. "After Barbara died, Noelle refused to leave home, and I'm afraid I didn't try very hard to persuade her. She enrolled here instead and continued to live with John and me."

A look of comprehension crossed his face. "Mmm, I see what you mean. She insisted that her brother and I needed her, and she was right. I guess she did sort of slip into the role of lady of the house. She kept things running smoothly and saw to it that Johnny and I ate properly and got enough sleep."

She didn't want him blaming himself for his daughter's possessiveness toward him. It could hardly have been avoided under the circumstances. "I understood from the conversation at lunch that she lives at a sorority house now."

"Yes, she does. Several of her friends had been after her to join, and last year Johnny and I finally convinced her that she should. She's in and out of here a lot, though, and we talk on the phone nearly every day."

Kirsten frowned. It was even worse than she'd thought. No wonder Noelle had resented her. Poor Court. He was in for a bad time if he ever did decide to marry again, even if only for companionship. From what she'd seen of his daughter, it was apparent that Noelle wasn't going to easily relinquish her role as the most important woman in her father's life.

Kirsten knew that if she valued her relatively trouble-free existence, she'd stay as far away as she could get from Courtney Forrester. She was much too attracted to him, and there were too many obstacles in their path. Better to turn back now before she got badly hurt.

Picking up her purse, Kirsten stood and tried for a lighter tone. "If we're scheduled to tour another child-care center we'd better be getting along."

As they drove back to the city after leaving the estate, Court returned to the subject of his daughter. "You disapproved of my giving Noelle money for the dress she wanted, didn't you?" he asked.

Kirsten sighed. "Court, the way you treat your daughter is none of my business."

He glanced at her. "That's true, but by asking the question I'm inviting your opinion. I noticed the look of disapproval on your face when she told Faith about it. Surely you get around your father the same way Noelle gets what she wants from me."

Kirsten bristled. "No, I don't. Neither do my two sisters. We were put on a moderate allowance as soon as we were old enough to handle money, and if we ran out before the end of the month we simply did without. We learned quickly to make sure that didn't happen."

Court turned and looked at her with disbelief. "But Dane could afford to bail you out."

"Sure he could," she snapped, stung by the implied criticism of her generous father, "but that's not the point. He was teaching us to handle the money we would one day earn, and eventually inherit. He wanted us to be independent, and I'm darn glad he did. Both Ingrid and I learned to live on our salaries and not go running to Dad to cover our debts." She grinned. "Ruth Anne is still struggling with that lesson, but she's only sixteen. She's learning fast that if she wants an eight-hundred-dollar dress she'd better budget her allowance for it."

Court chuckled. "I gather you're familiar with Dominique's prices."

Kirsten laughed, too. "Darn right I am. Her creations are gorgeous, but the few dresses I've bought there have been paid for in installments out of my salary. I didn't even mention the subject to Dad and Mom.''

His happier mood vanished, and he seemed to draw into himself. ''Barbara was good at disciplining the kids. She put them on allowances, too, and made them toe the mark, but after she died so suddenly...''

Kirsten had wondered about his wife's death. Women in their thirties usually didn't die from natural causes. ''Was she in an accident?'' she asked softly.

He shook his head. ''No, at least not the kind you're thinking of. It was a bee sting. She'd had mild allergic reactions in the past, and we kept epinephrine injection kits at home and in both our cars, but this time we'd borrowed the new Corvette we'd bought for Noelle as a high school graduation present. We were attending a barbecue and swim party at the ranch of a friend. Barb had just gotten out of the pool and was walking on the lawn in her bare feet when she stepped in a cluster of bees...''

His voice broke and he paused for a moment, then continued. ''She was stung several times. With no epinephrine available she died before we could get help. We found out later that there was a high concentration of clover in the grass.''

Kirsten's first instinct was to touch him, but she remembered that she'd done that once before and he'd misunderstood. ''How tragic,'' she said instead.

''Yes, it was.'' There was a quaver in his tone. ''It was the suddenness that made it so difficult for us to accept. If she'd been sick a long time or...'' He cleared his throat. ''Anyway, afterward I couldn't bring myself to deny Noelle and John anything. They'd suffered such a devastating loss.''

''Of course,'' Kirsten murmured. ''I'm sorry if I sounded judgmental. You've obviously done a marvelous job of being both father and mother to them. It's a tremendously difficult task.''

They rode in silence until they arrived at the next day-care center on their list.

Court was subdued and strictly business for the rest of the afternoon. The center they visited was mediocre and crowded to capacity, with the usual long waiting list. Afterward they went back to the factory and parted after arranging to meet again the next afternoon.

That night the feeling of dejection that had gnawed at Kirsten since her encounter with Court's daughter left her restless and made it difficult for her to sleep. During the long hours she was forced to face the fact that she was falling in love with Courtney Forrester, and she couldn't afford to let that happen.

Before meeting Noelle, she'd been confident that she could overcome his problems with the difference in their ages, the office romance awkwardness and even the lingering grief he felt for his late wife. Kirsten knew that if his feelings for her had any depth, those obstacles could be worked out, but how could she fight his daughter's opposition?

She couldn't. If she were only partially right about Noelle's possessive love for her father, Kirsten wouldn't even try. It would tear Court apart, and in the end she'd lose. Court wouldn't alienate his children, nor would she want him to.

Reluctantly she vowed to start looking for a position somewhere else.

The following morning Kirsten kept to her regular morning routine since Court had been unable to schedule an appointment to tour the on-site day-care center he'd found until after lunch.

By two o'clock her naturally bright and cheerful disposition had reasserted itself to some extent and she was feeling better. No matter how often she reminded herself to cool it, she couldn't stay depressed when she knew Court was coming for her. Just the thought of seeing him again and spending a few hours in his company made her shiver with delight.

She put the papers she was working on in a drawer and took out a mirror. A touch-up to her makeup gave her a fresh look that belied her lack of sleep.

Kirsten had worn a leaf-green suit with a lime silk blouse. She'd taken off the jacket while working alone in her office, and just as she stood up to reach for it there was a tap on the door and Court walked in.

His gaze collided with hers and locked. A surge of joy splashed through her and culminated in a wide and happy smile. She started toward him and then she was in his arms, swept into a hard, passionate embrace that left her breathless as his mouth took possession of hers.

The past twenty-two miserable hours were washed away on a tide of relief with the knowledge that he wanted her as much as she wanted him. Right now nothing mattered but her body pressed so intimately against his, his mouth plundering the dark, moist cavern of her own, and the touch of his hands wandering down her back to the taut rise of her derriere, then back again to stroke the sides of her full breasts.

She clasped her arms around his waist and clung, nipping his invading tongue gently with her teeth, and exploring the flexing muscles of his back through his suit coat. The future wasn't important; it was only the present that mattered. She hoped he'd go on kissing her forever.

When they finally tore apart they were both gasping. Kirsten could feel Court's heart beating against his chest, and knew her own was just as erratic.

He buried his face in her hair. "Oh, Kirsten, what am I going to do about you?" he groaned.

"What do you want to do about me?" She rubbed her cheek against the rough material of his suit.

"Don't ask," he said, then pushed her hips against him in such a way as to show her exactly what he wanted to do with her. "I feel as if I've been poleaxed and it has addled my brain. I can't figure out what happened. I neither needed nor wanted another special woman in my life, but then you walked into my office and I began to yearn."

His hands rested on the rise at the base of her spine, sending splinters of desire clawing through her.

"We couldn't have been more wrong for each other," he continued, "and I vowed to ignore that yearning. It worked pretty well until you touched me. My control crumbled and I clung to your warmth. Then when I kissed you... Oh, God, sweetheart, when I kissed you I was lost. Now I can't get you out of my mind, or worse, out of my heart."

Kirsten's spirits soared with every word. Maybe there was hope for them after all. She slid her arms up his back and crossed them around his neck as she raised her head and kissed him on the pounding pulse just under his jaw.

"You'll notice I'm not fighting you off," she said, and moved her lips to the other side of his face. "I'm just as lost as you are, but it doesn't bother me. I don't understand why the difference in our ages is so important to you."

One of his hands moved up to again caress her breast, making her ache for him to unfasten her blouse and bra, to feel his touch against her bare flesh.

"It may not seem all that important now," he said, his voice raspy, "but when you're my age I'll be in my sixties."

She strained against his palm as her nipple tightened under his stroking. "So what?" Her tone was barely above a whisper. "Look at Paul Newman. He's as vigorous and sexy as he was thirty years ago."

She heard a chuckle deep in his throat. "How would you know, my precious little love? You weren't even born thirty years ago. Besides, I'm not Paul Newman."

"So who wants Paul Newman if there's the faintest chance that they can have you?"

With a groan he kissed her again, but broke it off before it could become as compelling as before, and then released her and stepped away. "We'd better get out of here before I forget all my good intentions," he said, and reached for the doorknob.

Kirsten couldn't help wishing that he would forget most of his hang-ups about her, but she wasn't going to entice him into something he'd regret later. Instead she straightened her blouse, put on her jacket and walked out of the office with him.

Their destination was an electronics company known as a pioneer in test equipment. Court's secretary had scheduled an interview for them with Lloyd Oliver, president and one of the founders of the company.

When they were escorted into his office Kirsten was delighted to discover that he was a man in his late sixties with white hair and bifocals. Since most of the opposition to working mothers came from people in this age group, she felt that the fact he was setting up a day-care center on his grounds would have a positive influence on Court, who was young enough to be his son.

Mr. Oliver greeted them with a big smile. "Court, good to see you. Hear you're still winning all kinds of awards for that personal computer of yours."

The two men shook hands. "Thanks, Lloyd, we're doing okay. Maybe someday we'll be as successful as you." He turned to Kirsten. "I'd like you to meet my assistant personnel manager, Kirsten Anderson."

Kirsten put out her hand and it was engulfed in the man's bigger one. "It's an honor, Ms. Anderson. Please, sit down, both of you."

He motioned across the room to a gleaming leather sofa, and Court and Kirsten sat down together while he settled in a matching easy chair. "Now, what can I do for you?"

"Kirsten and I are looking into the possibility of setting up a day-care center in the new wing we're building at Evergreen," Court said, "and I was told that you're in the process of opening one. We'd like to talk to you about it."

The older man scowled. "If you're asking for advice, I can give it to you in one word. Don't."

Kirsten's muscles jerked with shock and surprise. What on earth could have gone wrong to make him so emphatic?

"I can give you more good advice, too," he continued. "Don't bring Johnny into your business until you're sure he's not going to be influenced by every pretty woman who bats her eyes at him."

Both Kirsten and Court snapped to attention, and Kirsten's jaws clenched. It was all she could do not to moan with despair. This man was going to destroy all her arguments.

"Oh, come on now, Lloyd..." Court began, but the other man wasn't about to be distracted.

"In my case it was a grandson, Paul's oldest boy," he continued heatedly. "He's been working for us as a trainee, and some of the women in assembly got hold of him. They gave him a sob story about their babysitting problems. Told him how great it would be if we had a nonprofit day-care center right here on the premises."

He paused, and Court quickly commented, "But I understood that the decision had been made to proceed with it. In fact, I was under the impression that it was about ready to open."

Lloyd waved his hand as if disposing of a troublesome bug. "That's probably the gist of the rumors that are going around. You know how out of hand things can get. I was on the yacht recuperating from surgery at the time, and my son Paul was acting president so the kid took it up with him."

With an anxious glance at Kirsten, Court again interrupted. "That's right, you had a heart attack earlier this year. Is everything all right now?" His concern was genuine, but he also seemed to be trying to change the subject.

Lloyd nodded. "Fine. They did a quadruple bypass, and Evelyn insisted that we take a cruise around the world while I was convalescing. Damn near died of boredom, but the ticker's good as new. Anyway, Paul decided the idea had merit and was actually having plans drawn up when I finally got back to work. Hell of a good thing I did, too, or he'd have bankrupted the company."

This time Kirsten had to speak up or explode. "Mr. Oliver! How on earth did you come to that conclusion?"

He turned his attention to her, looking surprised that she'd interrupted. "Very easily, my dear. I simply compared the cost with the return. There's no way in hell we'd ever get out of the red, and I'm not in business to lose money."

She saw Court frown and reach out to warn her, but she wouldn't be silenced. "You make it up in other ways," she argued.

"Such as?" he snapped.

Kirsten was ready for the question. "Increased productivity. When parents don't have to worry about their children they work harder and longer, have less absenteeism, take less emergency leave..."

She went over all the advantages on her long list, but instead of impressing him he only became more adamant.

"Look, Ms. Anderson, I expect my employees to work up to full capacity without me babysitting their kids." His tone was hard and inflexible. "I'm running a business, not a welfare agency. I pay them well and give them all the normal benefits, but I'm damned if I'm going to mollycoddle them. If women are going to have babies they should stay home and take care of them. If they want to work, then it's up to them to arrange for their own child care."

Oh my God! Kirsten wanted to scream and throw something. Lloyd Oliver sounded just like Court. Worse, because at least Court was willing to concede that men should do their share in raising their children.

She took a firm grip on herself and spoke slowly. "But apparently your son felt that the day-care center was a good idea since he'd approved it."

"Ha!" The sharp expletive was filled with scorn. "Paul never could say no to those three sons of his. He'd have approved a brothel if one of them had suggested it. When I'm dead and he takes over he can run the company any way he wants, but until then I'm in charge. If the women don't like it they can always quit."

Kirsten's temper snapped and she rose majestically out of her chair, a scathing comeback forming in her mind, but Court was quicker. He stood and took her arm in a warning grip. "I'm sure Paul thought he was making the right decision," he said softly to the older man. "And I'm equally sure that your doctor doesn't want you getting all riled up. Sorry if we upset you, Lloyd." He gripped the other man's hand. "Good to see you looking so fit and healthy. Ask Paul to call me when he can break away for a round of golf. Haven't seen him around the country club lately."

"I'll do that," Lloyd said heartily. "May even join the two of you if you don't mind. The doctor says I'm to exercise regularly."

Drawing on all the dignity at her command, Kirsten also put out her hand. "Thank you for giving us so much of your valuable time, Mr. Oliver." Her tone was cool but polite.

Lloyd took her hand. "It was my pleasure," he said. "Hope I've been some help."

Help! She'd have been happy if he just hadn't done so much harm!

Again they rode in strained silence on the way back to the plant. Kirsten wondered how much longer she could stand this wildly fluctuating relationship with Court. She was constantly riding the heights or plummeted to the depths of her emotions.

This morning she'd been depressed. Then Court had taken her in his arms and she'd soared with delight. Now, less than two hours later, she was in an agony of suspense. He was sitting behind the steering wheel so quiet and withdrawn.

Was he angry at her for arguing with his friend and business associate? Was he upset with Oliver for the way he'd talked to her? Or did he agree with Oliver that the whole day-care problem was not something he wanted to deal with?

A short time later, Court swung the car into the executive parking facility under the building. He glanced at the digital clock on the dash and grimaced, then turned to Kirsten. "I know we have to talk about this, but I have an appointment in ten minutes that can't be rescheduled. Will you have dinner with me tonight? We can discuss it then."

Kirsten couldn't expect him to take any more time away from his busy schedule. Still, she could see that he was influenced by Lloyd Oliver's stand, and she didn't want to try to refute his arguments in a public restaurant.

"I'd like to have dinner with you," she said, "but it's my turn to treat. Would you mind if we ate at my place? I'm a good cook, honest. I can even do gourmet if that's what turns you on."

Too late she realized that her last statement sounded flippant, if not downright suggestive, but Court laughed. "It's not your cooking that turns me on, honey," he said, and put his arms around her. "But I'd be very happy to have dinner with you at your place. Is eight o'clock too late?"

She snuggled against him. It was such a relief to know that he wasn't angry. "Eight's fine," she murmured as his lips caressed her temples. "Do you know where I live?"

"I'll find it, sweetheart. Believe me. Do I get a goodbye kiss?" His voice was low and husky.

She stroked his cheek. "Do you have time?"

"I'll make time," he whispered, and lowered his head.

Kirsten left work a little earlier than usual in order to stop at the market on her way home. She had butterflies in her stomach and felt like a teenager fixing dinner for her first boyfriend.

Although she knew she wasn't as sophisticated as many of her friends, she was no novice in the give and take of dating. She'd never lacked for escorts, and often entertained them in her home, both alone and with other couples. She was content with her high standards and her moral principles.

Kirsten had never considered herself in love before. No other man had electrified her the way Court Forrester did. She hadn't been prepared for the tingling of her nerve ends that his touch set off.

More important, though, was the tenderness she felt for him. The caring. The desire to comfort when he was sad, soothe when he hurt and protect him from further pain and sadness.

These emotions ran deep and frightened her. Court certainly didn't need her protection or her comfort. He was a strong man, quite capable of taking care of himself as well as his family and his electronics empire. He had a son and daughter who would no doubt always be there for him if he wanted emotional support.

Kirsten knew he didn't need her. Oh, he was attracted, all right, but he'd made it plain that she wasn't the type of woman he wanted in his life. Still she blossomed when he smiled and melted when he held her.

She was setting herself up for a lot of grief, but she couldn't bear to give up. Her nature was to decide what she wanted and then go after it. So far it had always worked, but her goal had never before been so impossible or the stakes so high.

Tonight, for the first time in months, she decided to show off her talent as a gourmet cook. Humming happily, she sautéed medallions of veal and blended the green peppercorn butter that would be added to them just before serving. The poached artichoke hearts filled with chopped wilted spinach took longer to prepare, but she could do that while the fall fruit crisp she'd fixed for dessert was baking. Later, she'd serve that warm with ice cream.

After setting the table in the dining room with her best silver, china and crystal, she showered and changed into a lavender outfit consisting of pajamalike pants and a thigh-length tunic tied loosely at the waist with a long belt. The neckline was cut in a V, and with it she wore several silver chains of various lengths and weights.

The effect was very sexy and feminine, a totally different look from the prim, tailored suits she wore to the office. She hoped it would knock Court's socks off, so to speak.

At a few minutes before eight, Court pulled up in front of Kirsten's address. There were spotlights hidden in the bushes that lit the whole front of the house. He could see that it was a zero-baseline condominium, a condo with no connecting walls. It was two-story, no more than four or five years old and newly painted in beige and brown. He'd guess it was in a high price range. Unless her father had bought it for her, and he strongly doubted that, she had to have been good at budgeting in order to make the payments on it.

He gathered up the long, narrow florist's box and the fancy plastic bag from the liquor store and walked up to the front door.

She answered on the first ring, and Court had to stifle a gasp when he saw her. He'd steeled himself to resist her beauty, and the pull of attraction that always drew him to her, but this was a different woman altogether.

Gone was the cool, professional demeanor, the tailored, understated clothes and the controlled hairstyle. In their place was a soft little temptress who took his breath away. Her brown hair swirled around her face and neck in a riot of curls, and her only discernible makeup was a touch of lip color and mascara.

She seemed shorter, and he realized it was because she'd discarded her high-heeled pumps for soft, flat slippers that matched the incredibly sexy outfit she wore. It was the color of passion, and the soft material shimmered, or maybe it was the natural glow of the gently rounded body beneath it that made his head swim.

His beautiful, efficient Kirsten had turned into an earthy sprite, glamorous and achingly desirable, and it was all he could do not to drop his packages and carry her off to the nearest bed.

It was apparent that she had no idea of the impact she'd made on him as she smiled and stood back. "Hi," she said. "Come on in. Dinner's almost ready."

He managed to pull himself together and greet her as he walked in, still clutching the box and bag.

Court followed her across a small entryway and hall into a rectangular, open-ended kitchen. At one end was the dining room and at the other what looked like a den or family room with a fireplace. He'd noticed the living room that jutted out at the front of the house when he came in.

He finally gained enough confidence in his control to set the bag on the counter and hand her the flower box. "Here," he said. "These are for you."

She opened it, and the shy smile she gave him when she saw the dozen white long-stemmed roses made him wish he'd brought a truckload. "Thank you, Court," she said in that breathless way she had of talking when something affected her deeply. "I don't believe I've ever had white roses before. They're magnificent."

She buried her face in the blossoms, and he wished it was him she was nuzzling.

He'd chosen white for purity. It was unlikely that at age twenty-five she was still a virgin, but she had an innocence about her that made the reality unimportant. Whatever her physical state, she was still unawakened to the miracle of the unity of body and soul; he'd stake his life on it.

In an effort to keep his hands off her he turned away and took the two bottles out of the bag. "I also brought wine. One's a Pinot Noir, and the other's a French Sauternes. I didn't know which you'd prefer so I brought them both."

She gave him a glowing look that told him she couldn't have been happier if he'd brought her the fountain of youth. "We'll use them both. The Pinot Noir with dinner, and the Sauternes with dessert. If you'd like to chill them there's a silver bucket in the top right cupboard and ice in the fridge."

Kirsten arranged the white roses and green fern in a ruby cut crystal vase while Court packed the wine bottles in ice cubes. When they'd finished, she put the flowers on the table, then walked over to Court and put her arms around him. "It was sweet and thoughtful of you to bring me gifts," she murmured just before she kissed him square on the mouth.

He was surprised at her boldness in initiating an embrace, but his gratitude and pleasure knew no bounds. She'd always responded to him, but until now he'd had to make the first move.

His arms closed around her waist, and she was all curves and fragrance and smooth, slippery satin. *Careful,* he reminded himself as his mouth moved against hers. *She's very young. Don't take more than you're willing to give back.*

Chapter Six

It was a noble thought, but as Kirsten's tongue shyly circled Court's lips and begged entry, his caution went up in smoke and he opened to her gentle probing. His hungry hands slid over the sensual fabric of her garment and made contact with the curves underneath. His imagination soared as he pictured her high breasts, tiny waist and firm, round bottom nude in his arms.

Oh, how he wanted her, and not just in his bed. He was becoming positively obsessed with this fascinating young woman. In the mornings he longed to see her across the breakfast table from him, in the evenings he imagined her sitting in the den with him, reading or watching television, or maybe feeding a contented dark-haired baby snuggled at her full breast...

The idea jolted him so severely that he broke off the kiss. Good grief, where had that thought come from? He was in worse shape than he'd realized.

A baby? He had no intention of getting involved with a woman young enough to want children. He was too old to start another family!

Kirsten blinked with surprise and searched Court's face. Why had he pulled away from her so suddenly? He'd seemed as engrossed in their kiss as she was, but now he looked startled, almost shocked.

"Is—is something wrong?" she stammered.

He still held her loosely, but it seemed to take a moment for him to focus on her question. When he did he cradled her to him again and bussed her lightly on the forehead. "Wrong?" he asked softly. "No, but you're an extremely tempting armful, and my self-control is limited. I think we'd better eat."

She smiled with relief and the purely female satisfaction of knowing that the man in her life wanted her so badly.

She grinned and disengaged herself from him. "Oh, all right," she said and pouted. "If you'd rather eat than..."

He put a finger across her lips, stilling her. "I'm warning you, love." His tone was serious, but his eyes shone with amusement. "Hunger can be a compelling urge, and I'm ravenous."

She knew he wasn't talking about food, and she also understood that although he spoke lightly, he was telling her the truth. She shivered with the desire to throw herself into his arms and give him what he so desperately needed, what she so passionately wanted, but with the last remnant of her good sense she resisted.

It was too soon. Not for her, but he was still fighting the attraction between them. He wasn't ready for the commitment that making love to her would impose on an honorable man like Court. He'd blame himself afterward, then feel responsible for her. Kirsten didn't want that kind of relationship. He had to come to her freely, with no doubts or regrets, or without ever meaning to, he'd break her reckless, loving heart.

She reached up and put her hand over his, then kissed the finger that still caressed her mouth. "I guess we'd better settle for food." She realized that her disappointment sounded in her voice.

Taking a deep breath, she made a massive effort to lighten up as she turned toward the stove. "Please hand me the log of peppercorn butter from the refrigerator. Dinner will be ready in five minutes."

By the time they'd finished the fruit crisp they'd gotten the conversation back on an impersonal track and were laughing and enjoying the food. Court put down his spoon and sighed. "I haven't enjoyed a meal this much in years," he said. "You're an excellent cook, Kirsten."

She smiled, happy with the compliment. "My mother wasn't one to let the long summers go to waste. She sent her daughters to private classes. I can cook, sew, garden, handle my personal finances and dance everything from ballet to punk rock."

Court laughed. "No wonder you're such a well-rounded lady. But how come she forgot to teach you how to change diapers?"

He was referring to their first meeting, and Kirsten howled with glee. "She did, but we practiced on dolls instead of babies. I never learned how to catch them, hold them and pin on the diapers with just two hands."

She pushed back her chair and stood. "Shall we have coffee in the family room?" She motioned to the room across the kitchen.

Court observed that the rooms in Kirsten's condo weren't large, but they were strategically placed and furnished to make use of every bit of space. The brick fireplace in the family room was flanked by a beige velour sofa, and on the other side by two thickly padded easy chairs in a medium shade of brown. An elaborate stereo and television system filled one wall, and the other looked into a glass-enclosed indoor atrium, softly lighted and colorful with exotic plants and blossoms.

"Why don't you take off your coat and loosen your tie?" Kirsten said as she curled up with her legs under her in the nearest big chair.

He wasn't sure that shedding any of his clothes was a good idea, but her invitation was too tempting to resist.

He removed the navy suede sport coat and tossed it across the back of the sofa, then sat down at the end across from Kirsten. He left his white shirt buttoned at the throat, and his tie in place, knowing that he didn't dare relax too far.

The glow from the fire and the muted light from the atrium were the only illumination in the room. The setting was peaceful and quiet, and dangerously seductive.

It took all of Court's concentration to drag his gaze away from Kirsten and bring up the subject he knew would again plunge them into a battle of opposing views. "I'm sure you have an opinion about Lloyd Oliver's stand on child care in the workplace. Would you care to discuss it?"

The soft, contented look on her lovely face was replaced by one of disgust. "You're darn right I have an opinion," she said angrily. "The man's forty years behind the times. He still thinks of women as household drudges."

Court couldn't help but smile. "I hardly think you'd call his wife, Evelyn, a drudge. She's never held a paying job, but she's given countless hours of her time to heading up charity drives. Evelyn is a skillful fund-raiser."

Kirsten set her cup down on the table beside her. "I know all about Mrs. Oliver's good works, and I admire her very much, but that doesn't alter the fact that she's serving without salary because she can afford to. She has more money than she can ever spend. The majority of the women who work today are barely making ends meet, even on two paychecks. Why can't her husband see that?"

"Now you're the one who's being unfair," Court protested heatedly. "Children are the responsibility of their parents, not the community. Businesses are under no obligation to provide babysitting for their employees. Lloyd's right, there's no way that an on-site day-care center would ever pay for itself. It would always be a financial drain, and you'll never convince me that's sound economic judgment."

Kirsten swung her feet to the floor and sat up straight, the gleam of battle in her eyes. "You just refuse to listen to me, dammit. I've told you, you make it up in other ways."

Court stood and ran his hand through his hair in frustration. This intelligent woman who looked like an angel, thought like an activist and spoke like a rebel was going to drive him mad. She aroused his passion and his temper with equal ease, and he never knew from one minute to the next if she was going to impel him to make love to her or to fire her.

"Oh, I listen to you." His tone was harsh and low. "I'm impossibly behind schedule because I've spent so much time listening to you and trying to please you, but so far I haven't found a compelling reason to change things. I've never had labor-relations problems, and I don't anticipate that I will unless you stir them up over this day-care issue."

Kirsten jumped to her feet. "Are you accusing me of causing dissension?" There was outrage in her tone.

For a moment he was tempted to placate her, to do or say anything to get back into her good graces, but he knew that would just be a delaying tactic. This issue had to be faced and battled out, and it might as well be now.

"No," he said. "At least, not yet, but there's a real danger that you will if word of your request gets around the plant and then I veto it. You believe passionately in what you're crusading for, and I respect that, but you're losing sight of one unsavory element of this whole thing."

She looked startled. "I don't know what you mean."

He took a deep breath and plunged ahead. "Kirsten, you keep telling me that today's woman wants to be independent. That she can take care of herself and doesn't need a man to support her. That she can have it all, career, marriage and children, without giving up anything. But, sweetheart, you're not facing the fact that in petitioning business, either private sector or government, to be responsible for the children, women are not being self-sufficient. They're transferring their dependence from the man in their life to the government."

Even in the dim light Court could see the blood drain from Kirsten's face. "That . . . that's not true," she stammered, but the certainty that had throbbed in her voice before was gone.

He reached out and cupped her shoulders. "Yes it is, and the power goes with the money. If I'm going to lose money by underwriting child care in my plant, then I'm going to insist on control. Any businessman would. We all have stockholders and boards of directors to answer to, and they'd demand it."

"No," she whispered.

"Yes. As I've said all along, someone has to raise the children. If mothers relinquish that role to their employers, then the employers are going to have the final say in how the children are cared for. Believe it."

Kirsten felt as if she'd had all the props knocked out from under her. With every ounce of strength she wanted to deny Court's reasoning, but what he said made sense. Was she encouraging these working mothers to give up one form of domination only to become ensnared by another?

He put his arm around her and led her toward the couch. "Come on, honey, let's sit down and talk, calmly and reasonably."

He pulled her down with him and cradled her in his arms. It felt so good to lean against him, her head on his shoulder, his hand caressing her hip. She wished she'd never gotten involved in the explosive subject of child care. But Court would never have taken an interest in her if she hadn't had a cause that brought her to his attention.

During all the time she'd worked at Evergreen, there'd never been a hint of gossip about the head of the company and any of his women employees.

Court brushed his lips across Kirsten's forehead and into her soft, fragrant hair. The rational part of him screamed warnings, but his overwhelming maleness demanded relief from the aching need to hold her, kiss her ripe, willing lips, caress the curves that seemed to strain for his touch.

What could it hurt? He was long past the age of being ruled by his baser instincts. He could control both himself and the situation. All he wanted was the closeness, the caring, the thrill of a little light lovemaking. He wouldn't compromise her. A romantic encounter didn't always have to end up in bed.

"I love the way you cuddle against me, so soft and warm and trusting." His tone was laced with tenderness. "It's lonesome in that big house of mine all by myself. I like this place of yours. It's small but homey. The kind of retreat where you can be alone but not lonely."

"I'm glad you approve," she said, and reached up to unfasten the button under his tie. "It took me a long time to find it, but when I did I knew it was what I was looking for."

"How many bedrooms do you have?" He had trouble keeping his voice steady as her fingers tackled the second button and sent shivers down his spine.

"Three. I don't need that many, but Dad said just two bedrooms isn't a good investment."

How did she manage to keep up a rational conversation and drive him half out of his mind at the same time? "Your father would know after all his years as a realtor."

"Yes," she said absently. "Do you mind if I take off your tie? You'd be more comfortable without it."

Fleetingly he wondered if she had any idea what she was doing to him. "Sweetheart, you can undress me as far as you want, but if you get past the tie you'd better be prepared to take the consequences." His voice was raspy and he cleared his throat.

"If you'd rather I didn't..." She started to take her hand away.

He captured it and held it against his chest. "Please don't stop. I want you to remove my tie, and anything else your little heart desires."

Her big brown eyes were filled with uncertainty. "I don't mean to tease..."

He bent his head and kissed the tip of her nose. "Take off the tie, Kirsten," he said quietly.

It took both hands for her to loosen the knot and slide it from under his collar. "Now, unbutton the rest of my shirt and put your hands underneath it."

Without hesitation she did as he asked, and the touch of her palms against his bare chest made him shiver.

She looked up at him with a question in those beautifully expressive eyes, and he smiled. "It's all right," he assured her. "That's the way your touch affects me, but I can control it."

The hell you can, you idiot.

It was an unwelcome voice from deep inside him, and he quickly shut it out. Kirsten was a grown woman. She was old enough to know what she was doing when she'd started this.

And you're old enough to know that the kind of fire the two of you are building can't always be doused before it's too late to prevent a conflagration, the persistent voice within insisted.

Kirsten's fingers wove back and forth through the dense growth of hair on his chest, and she laid her cheek against his heated flesh, driving out all caution as he clutched her to him. Surely he was entitled to a little happiness. The only other woman who'd ever stirred his soul as well as his passion was Barbara, and he'd been existing in an emotional wasteland since her death. Was it really so wrong to give in to the compelling need Kirsten kindled in him? The need for love as well as sex?

He found the hem of her tunic and slowly tugged it upward until he could slide his hand underneath. It encountered warm, bare skin, and this time it was her muscles that contracted. She drew in her breath and exhaled its sweet breeze against his own skin, which was already sensitized by the pressure of her cheek.

His heart seemed to skip a beat as he inched farther until his palm covered her rib cage. She was slender but nicely padded, and she felt smooth and pliant as her chest rose and fell with her accelerated breathing.

He paused, afraid to continue his exploration for fear she'd pull away, but of their own volition his long fingers turned and stretched until they made contact with the firm rise of her breast. A mixture of textures, the smoothness of satin and the stiffer cutwork of lace, provided a barrier to the sensual contact of her bare flesh against his hand.

Although frustrating, it was probably just as well. He already had about all the stimulation he could handle.

He cupped her lightly supported breast and forced himself to stop with that. He still had his wits about him even though her hands were sending pinpricks of almost unbearable pleasure all through him as they roamed over his chest and occasionally wandered to his navel and slightly below.

It was Kirsten who broke the spell with words. "Court."

Her voice had a husky, slumberous timbre.

"Mmm." He didn't really want to talk.

"Will you still consider the day-care center?"

It was like being knifed in the back when you least expected it. Court was jolted to reality, and the pain was excruciating.

All the time he'd thought they were both caught up in the wonder of mutual passion she'd been conniving to keep him from dropping the day-care project.

For a moment he sat absolutely still, afraid even to breath as the anguish sliced through him. Then he slowly withdrew his hand from beneath her blouse and straightened, although he still cuddled her to him with his other arm.

She raised up to look at him. "Court?" She must have seen the disillusionment that he knew was plainly stamped on his face. "What's the matter?"

She actually looked puzzled, and that was the cruelest jab of all. Did she honestly think he was too naive to know when he was being seduced? It had been tried by women a lot older, wiser and more experienced than she without success.

Damn! He'd begun to hope that this time...

He raised the arm that held her and moved away so he could put it down at his side. "There's nothing you won't do to get what you want, is there?"

She appeared even more perplexed. "Wh-what do you mean?"

He'd almost swear from her expression that she was hurt by his abrupt withdrawal. Well, possibly she was. She did seem to be attracted to him. Maybe she saw nothing wrong with her little game. After all, who was he to object? He'd arranged his share of trade-offs on his climb to the top.

He stood and picked up his jacket. "Never mind," he said dispassionately. "It's my own fault. I should have known..."

"Should have known what?" Kirsten stood also, a frown marring her smooth brow.

He put the coat on and jammed the tie in his pocket. "I should have remembered that you're only trying to do your job, which is to keep my employees content and productive. If playing up to the old man will take his mind off the obstacles and smooth the way for a project you truly believe will accomplish that, then why not?"

She gasped, and looked as if he'd hit her. "You can't mean that."

He turned away, afraid she'd see how badly she'd hurt him. "Lighten up, honey," he said, fighting to keep his tone impersonal. "You've just learned a valuable lesson. Us over-forty guys aren't as gullible or as harmless as you seem to think. I know you wouldn't have let it go all the way with me, but next time you might not have a choice. I'm sure you've heard that old chestnut, 'just because there's snow on the roof doesn't mean the fire's gone out in the furnace.'"

Anger was replacing the pain, and when he turned once more to face her he was in control of himself and the situation. His tone was no longer impersonal but deadly serious. "There's plenty of fire left in my furnace, Kirsten, and I'm an expert at playing rough. Don't push me too far."

He started to walk toward the entryway but her soft, compelling voice stopped him. "You're wrong, Court. I would have let it go all the way with you. If you'd wanted me badly enough to keep your nasty suspicions to yourself, I'd have taken you upstairs to bed with me."

A jagged groan was torn from the knot of agony in his gut. "Ah, love, you still don't understand, do you? It was because I wanted you so badly that I couldn't let that happen.''

He strode to the door and disappeared into the dark.

Kirsten was late for work the next morning, and she felt like a battered and bloody battleground. The analogy wasn't altogether inaccurate. She'd been battling internally and all it had gotten her was a sleepless night and a pounding headache.

For a long time after Court had left she'd stood there in a trance, hearing his last words bouncing off the walls. *It was because I wanted you so badly that I couldn't let that happen.*

Why wouldn't he trust her? This was the second time he'd accused her of coming on to him in order to get that daycare center. The first occasion was understandable; he'd known her only a short while and he'd had the experience before.

But now they knew each other, had even been close. How could he still think that she'd do something so despicable?

It had taken her a long time to figure that one out. He'd been right, there was a generation gap between them. He'd been raised to believe that "nice girls" waited for their dream man to find them and give them everything they needed.

She, on the other hand, had never waited for anyone to get things for her. She'd always gone after what she wanted. That's the way she'd acquired her education and her career, and when she'd realized that Court was the man she wanted in her life, she'd gone after him, too.

Thinking back on the events of the day, she finally understood how he'd arrived at such a grossly mistaken conclusion.

It had started with Lloyd Oliver's negative attitude. Court had known she was upset, and had even asked her to go out to dinner with him so they could talk about it.

That's where she'd made her first mistake. She'd convinced him to have dinner at her home instead. Then she'd made a private party of it with elegant food served on expensive china and crystal, when what he'd proposed was a business meal.

Even her clothes had been misleading. Instead of leaving on her suit, or changing into tailored slacks and a shirt, she'd donned a slinky, sexy outfit. When he'd reacted in a typical male way at the sight of her and kissed her so eagerly, she'd responded just as eagerly.

Finally the coup de grace. Her cheeks flamed even as she thought about it. While they were making out on the couch, after he'd told her in plain terms that he considered on-site day care not only a bad investment but a poor solution to the problem, her behavior had gone past responsive to positively wanton.

That was bad enough, but to have brought up the subject again just when they were close to the point of no return was an act of incredibly bad timing on her part. He had no way of knowing that she was desperately casting around for a subject to talk about in order to cool them both down a little and try to regain control of the situation. Their last conversation just happened to be the first thing that came to mind, and she'd spoken without thinking.

It was tactless, insensitive and stupid. No wonder Court thought he was being manipulated.

Kirsten knew she had to talk to him and try to straighten things out, but she didn't see or hear from him on Thursday. Several times she picked up the phone to call, but then put it down again. She didn't want to bother him when he was busy.

On Friday, after another restless night, she resolved to call him as soon as she got to the office.

The phone rang at the other end of the line and Tanya answered. "May I speak to Mr. Forrester, please," Kirsten asked in her most businesslike tone, hoping the secretary would not recognize her voice.

"I'm sorry, but Mr. Forrester won't be coming in today. Would you like to leave a message?"

Kirsten was caught off balance. "Oh. No, no message. Uh...could you tell me how I can get in touch with him?"

"I'm sorry. I don't have that information." Tanya's voice had become chilly. "Would you like to speak with Mrs. Warren, Mr. Forrester's executive secretary?"

Kirsten knew Wilma Warren. Middle-aged, frighteningly efficient, and a real dragon when it came to getting rid of unauthorized phone callers or visitors. "No," she answered hastily. "No, thank you. I'll try again next week."

By Saturday afternoon Kirsten was desperate. She had to find Court and try to explain. She couldn't let him go on thinking she'd treat him so shamelessly. He might not believe her, but she had to try.

But how? His home phone number was unlisted, and she didn't have it in her files. There was no need for her to. As an employee she'd have no reason to call him there.

The only way she could contact him was to go to his estate. Even if he wasn't there she could leave a message with Mrs. Underhill, asking him to call her.

At least he'd know she'd tried.

Without bothering to change out of her jeans and sweatshirt, she grabbed her purse and headed for the garage. She had only a hazy idea of how to get to the Forrester residence, but after several wrong turns she finally found the right road and followed it to the high fence, then on to the closed gates. She stopped at the gatehouse and rolled down her window.

A security guard came out and leaned down to look at her. "Your name, please," he said pleasantly.

In her anxiety she'd forgotten that she couldn't just drive right up to the house. "Kirsten Anderson," she said with a smile. "I'm here to see Mr. Courtney Forrester."

"Are you expected, ma'am?"

Her smiled dimmed. "Well, no, but it's important."

"Just a moment, please." He went back into the small enclosure and picked up a phone.

Kirsten fidgeted. Good grief, it was like visiting someone in prison.

She wasn't unfamiliar with security measures. Her own parents had an unlisted number, and a complete and sensitive home alarm system. Their neighbors did, too, but this was ridiculous. She couldn't imagine living behind locked gates.

The guard returned. "Sorry, Miss, but Mr. Forrester isn't in residence at this time."

In residence? Kirsten was about to ask just what the hell *in residence* meant when the sound of a fast-approaching vehicle was followed by the squeal of brakes as a white BMW convertible screeched to a stop directly behind her.

The man excused himself and hurried over to speak to the driver of the other car. Kirsten watched in the rearview mirror, and saw the door open and Court's daughter, Noelle, get out.

Kirsten felt trapped. All she'd wanted was to apologize to Court, but it seemed that he lived in a fortress and she had to go through an army of people to get to him. The last thing she needed was another go-round with the Forrester heiress.

If there had been any way to make a hasty exit she'd have just told the guard to forget it and driven away. Unfortunately there was a locked gate in front of her, a gleaming luxury car blocking the driveway behind and a security guard who wore a gun watching her suspiciously.

Chapter Seven

Noelle Forrester was dressed in tight designer jeans and a bulky sweater, with a brightly colored silk scarf tied over her long blond hair to keep it from blowing in the wind. She walked the few steps to Kirsten's Jaguar and leaned down to look at her. "Well, Ms. Anderson, we meet again. Bud says you want to see Dad. Is it something I can help you with?"

She sounded friendly enough, but her gaze was coldly speculative.

Kirsten shook her head. "No, thank you, Noelle," she said, with what she hoped was just the right amount of hauteur. "As the officer said, it's your father I came to see."

Noelle's heavily made up blue eyes widened in a look of innocent surprise. "But Dad's on vacation. Didn't you know?"

Vacation? Court? But he hadn't said a thing...

Kirsten quickly masked her surprise and pulled her thoughts together. "No, I didn't. In that case I guess it will have to wait until he comes back." She hesitated. "Could you tell me when that will be?"

Noelle shrugged. "Haven't a clue. Look, as long as you're here why don't you come up to the house with me and have a drink? Guess it's about time we got better acquainted since you and Dad are such good friends."

Kirsten caught the thinly veiled sarcasm in the other woman's tone, and decided she'd better find out what Court's daughter was leading up to. "Thanks, I'd like that."

"Fine. Since you're in front you can lead the way. Just go through the gate and follow the road to the top of the hill."

"Yes, I know." Kirsten answered automatically, then could have bitten her tongue at Noelle's startled look. Obviously Court hadn't told her that Kirsten had been there before.

When they got to the house Noelle rang the bell. Mrs. Underhill answered and unlocked all the locks so they could enter.

"I've never been in a house that was so tightly secured as this one," Kirsten observed. "Is this all really necessary?"

"You're darn right it is," Noelle snapped. "You wouldn't believe how many threats are made against Dad. He doesn't talk about it, especially to Johnny and me, but we listened in one time when he was discussing it with the security people. When we were younger, Dad and Mom apparently lived in fear that we'd be kidnapped. They weren't taking any chances."

She pulled the scarf off her head and tossed it on a marble-top table in the foyer where they stood. "Let's go sit in the playroom. It's got a fully stocked wet bar." She stepped back and gestured. "You first."

Kirsten looked around her. "I don't know where it is."

Noelle looked genuinely surprised this time. "I thought you'd been here before."

Kirsten nodded. "I have, once, but . . ."

"You mean Dad rushed you upstairs to bed without even giving you a tour of the house first?" Noelle's tone was vicious.

Instinctively Kirsten raised her arm and started to swing at Noelle, but caught herself in time to stop. "If you ever talk to me that way again I'll jar your teeth loose and that's a promise," she snapped.

"You wouldn't dare," Noelle taunted. "I can have every law officer in the county here before you get to your car."

Kirsten was as surprised as Noelle by her behavior, and almost as appalled. She'd never hit anyone in anger, or even threatened to. She wasn't proud of her threat, but neither was she ashamed. Noelle had it coming and Kirsten wasn't going to either back down or apologize.

"I'm sure you can," she said in a tightly controlled tone. "Call out the National Guard if it'll make you happy, and if you don't mind the newspaper and television headlines."

Noelle stared at her uncomprehendingly. "You know," Kirsten continued, "the ones that read, Courtney Forrester's Daughter And Latest Girlfriend In Slugging Match! It won't matter to them that I'm not his girlfriend."

Noelle straightened up and sputtered, "Why, you... you..."

"Careful, doll," Kirsten grated, being deliberately coarse. "I fight my own battles, and you'd better not forget that. Now, if you'd like to lead the way to the playroom I think we have several things to talk over."

Noelle glared at her, then turned and stomped down a hall to the back of the house, where they entered a huge rectangular room with a spectacular view of the outdoors from two glass walls. One end was furnished as a sitting room, and the rest lived up to its name, "the playroom." There were two pool tables, a complete stereo system and a giant television set, and enough space in the middle for dancing. The sliding glass doors on the back wall led to a covered patio and an Olympic-size swimming pool with dressing rooms off to the side.

Noelle flounced over to the built-in bar. "What are you drinking?" Her tone was harsh.

"Whatever you're having," Kirsten answered dryly.

Noelle took two high-ball glasses from the cupboard and filled them with ice, then poured Scotch whiskey to the brim. Kirsten eyed them balefully, but said nothing as she took one and carried it across the room to the semicircular modular seating unit and sat down. Noelle followed behind her and sat at the opposite end.

Kirsten lost no time getting to the point. "Now that we understand each other, what did you want to talk about?"

Noelle took a swallow of her whiskey. "I want to know what's going on between you and my father?"

Kirsten raised one eyebrow. "That's none of your business."

"I'm making it my business. Women have been coming on to Dad ever since my mother died. It's disgusting the way they simper and drool over him. And you . . . you're a generation too young for him."

"That's what upsets you the most, isn't it?" Kirsten said quietly. "The fact that you and I are so nearly the same age."

"You're darn right it is." Noelle slammed her glass down on the sprawling redwood-burl coffee table. "Dad really gave me hell the day after we all had lunch together. He claimed I was rude to you. He says you're the daughter of the family that owns Anderson Realty."

Kirsten nodded. "That's right."

"Well, I've seen Dane Anderson on those television commercials he does. He's about Dad's age, and almost as good-looking. How would you feel if your mother had died recently and your dad started cozying up to a woman your age?'' She picked up her glass again and settled against the thickly upholstered back.

Kirsten's first reaction was to heatedly deny that her father would ever take up with another woman, young or middle-aged. She managed to bite back the comment, but she was shaken by the fierceness of her need to reject such an idea.

Her father and mother adored each other. They behaved more like newlyweds than an old married couple who had been together for over twenty-five years. Her father would never love another woman the way he loved his wife!

Or would he? Dane was still a young man. Would she expect him to spend the rest of his life alone? Was it possible that Kirsten Anderson had the potential to be every bit as jealous and possessive of her father as Noelle Forrester was of Court?

Kirsten cradled the crystal glass in her two hands and looked down at the dark clear liquid swirling among the ice cubes. ''I expect I'd feel the same way you do, Noelle,'' she said in answer to the other woman's question. ''And I'd be just as wrong as you are.''

''What do you mean, wrong?'' Noelle asked belligerently.

Kirsten shrugged. ''Just what I said. It would be wrong of either of us to assume we knew what was best for our fathers. Your mother didn't die recently, Noelle. It's been over three years now, and you and your brother and Court have to go on with your lives. She wouldn't want you to mourn forever.''

''You don't have any idea what she'd want!'' Noelle hissed, her tone irate. ''You didn't even know her.''

Kirsten silently cursed herself for her insensitivity and took a sip of her whiskey. ''You're right,'' she said carefully. ''I'm sorry. Now I'm the one who's assuming. You see how dangerous it can be. But to get on with the point I'm trying to make, it's not fair to insist that I'm young enough to be Court's daughter, too. There's only eighteen years difference in our ages. That's not a generation.''

Noelle eyed her with sullen disbelief. ''Plenty of eighteen-year-old boys get girls pregnant.''

''Sure they do,'' Kirsten agreed, ''but they're still boys, not men. A fourteen-year-old male is capable of fathering a child, but it doesn't make him a man. Court was twenty-two years old and had been married for a year when you were born. By that time I was four years old.''

She watched Noelle shake the ice in her glass and twirl the liquor around it before taking another shallow. ''You're nit-picking,'' she said angrily. ''The point is that if I ever do have a stepmother thrust on me, I sure don't want people mistaking her for my sister.''

Kirsten heard her own ice tinkling and realized that the hand that held her drink was trembling. She took another sip and grimaced. She didn't like the taste of whiskey.

''I can understand that,'' she said, ''but it's a moot point, anyway. Your father has no intention of getting involved with me. He's told me so on several occasions, the last one just before he left on vacation. I'll admit that I'm very, uh, fond of him, but seducing him against his will isn't my style, if that's what you're worried about. I doubt that I could do it, anyway. He's a very stubborn, strong-willed man.''

She put the glass down on the table and stood. ''Thanks for inviting me in.'' She bent over to pick up her shoulder bag from the floor. ''I'm afraid our little talk did more harm than good, though.''

Noelle stood, too. ''Oh, I don't know.'' A hint of a smile tugged at the corners of her mouth. ''If you weren't out to bewitch my Dad I might learn to like you.''

Kirsten raised one elegant eyebrow. ''That's good of you. If you weren't Court's spoiled-rotten daughter I think I might like you, too.''

* * *

For the next two weeks, Kirsten's spirits dropped steadily as each day went by without a word from Court. She felt hurt and betrayed that he hadn't mentioned to her that he was taking a vacation. They'd been together a lot in the two days before they'd quarreled, but he hadn't indicated that he'd be leaving immediately for an extended length of time.

Had he intended to make love to her and then just walk away? Had he been looking for an excuse to break off any personal relationship between them? Was he vacationing alone, or did he have a companion?

It was the last question that tormented her at night when she couldn't sleep.

When members of the day-care committee asked how the negotiations were coming, she had to tell them that everything was on hold for the time being because Mr. Forrester was out of town, but it looked like a lost cause. She was tempted to use the day-care thing as an excuse to question Tanya about his scheduled return, but didn't. It would only call attention to her curiosity and wouldn't get her any information.

Finally, toward the end of the second week, Kirsten contacted an employment agency that specialized in executive placements and asked them to find her a position with another company.

It nearly tore her apart, but she couldn't work for Court after he'd made it plain that she meant nothing to him. He was too much of a gentleman to fire her, but maybe if she were gone someone else could convince him to try the on-site day-care center.

On Friday she typed her letter of resignation and left it on the desk of her immediate supervisor, Marguerite. She'd given four weeks' notice, which meant she'd be leaving Evergreen about the middle of December.

She choked back a sob. Merry Christmas!

* * *

It seemed to Court that he'd had the drone of aircraft motors in his ears forever as he shifted restlessly. The seats in first class were wider and better padded than in tourist, but after fifteen hours or so in the air he was stiff and sore.

It was bad enough when he felt well, but the damned enteritis that had felled him for several days in Tokyo had struck again without warning about halfway through the flight, and he'd never been so miserable. He was alternately hot and cold, and his head felt like it was going to explode with the pain that beat and throbbed incessantly. At first he'd tried taking aspirin, but his stomach had immediately rebelled and set off a chain reaction that kept him running to the rest room until there was nothing left to come up.

Unfortunately that didn't discourage the waves of nausea that swept through him at regular intervals.

An involuntary groan escaped and brought the attendant to hover over him again. "Is there anything I can get you, Mr. Forrester?" she asked for the hundredth time. "If you can just hold on for another twenty minutes we'll be landing in San Francisco. Won't you reconsider and let us call for an ambulance?"

Court knew that having a medical emergency aboard an airplane flying over thousands of miles of water was a nightmare flight attendants dreaded, but he wished she'd just go away and leave him alone. Every time he felt her cool hand on his forehead, or heard her soft voice talking to him, he dared to hope it was Kirsten. In his stupor he'd even called her name once or twice, then been jolted back to reality when he'd opened his eyes.

Struggling not to sound impatient, he gave her the same answer he'd given her at least half a dozen times before. "No, please, no ambulance. I've had this before. I even have medication in my luggage. I'll be all right as soon as we land

and I can get some rest. You can tell me what day and time it is in San Francisco, though.''

She looked at her watch. ''It's 7:50 p.m. on Sunday,'' she said. ''If you need help deplaning, let me know.''

The red-eye night flight from San Francisco to Washington, D.C. was boarding as Kirsten hugged her father and kissed him. ''Try to get some sleep, Dad, so you'll be bright-eyed and alert when you meet with the senator in the morning.''

Dane's arms tightened around her. ''Yes, Mama,'' he said with a teasing grin. ''Thanks, honey, for driving me over. I'd hate to have to leave the car at the airport for a week. Be careful on the drive back to San Jose, though. Keep your doors locked and don't stop for anything.''

''Yes, Papa,'' she mimicked. ''Now run along before they take off without you.''

She kissed him again and watched until he disappeared down the ramp and into the plane.

As she walked rapidly up the concourse to the main lobby of San Francisco International Airport, Kirsten was debating whether to take the time to eat at the cafeteria or wait and fix dinner for herself at home. It was after eight now, and it would take her close to an hour to get there if luck was with her and there weren't any traffic tie-ups.

Absently she noticed a man in a wheelchair ahead of her being pushed up by a skycap and accompanied by a flight attendant. She quickened her pace and passed the wheelchair entourage, then hurried on ahead until she heard what sounded like her name.

She stopped, but before she could spin around a hand clutched her shoulder.

Kirsten turned and faced a uniformed flight attendant. ''Is your name Kirsten?'' the woman asked.

Kirsten blinked with surprise. ''Why, yes, but . . .''

"We have a passenger who says he knows you. Would you mind stepping over there for a minute?"

Kirsten looked where the attendant motioned and saw both the man in the wheelchair and the skycap off to the side out of the mainstream of traffic. There were too many people blurring her vision to make out his features, but she certainly wasn't expecting to see anyone she knew.

She must have hesitated longer than she'd intended because the other woman continued without waiting for an answer. "Please, ma'am, the gentleman is ill but he won't let us call an ambulance. We can't allow him to leave the airport without someone to take responsibility for him."

Kirsten nodded and followed the woman to the seating area where the wheelchair was parked. It wasn't until she was nearly there that she recognized Court, and then she ran.

He tried to stand, but she crouched down beside the chair and took both of his hands in hers. His were hot to the touch.

"Court, my God, what's happened?" It was a cry of terror.

He looked awful. His eyes were red-rimmed and had dark bruises under them. His face was drawn and flushed with fever, but he was shivering.

He didn't say anything, but withdrew his hands from hers and pulled her into his arms as close as he could get her with the hard metal of the chair between them. She put her arms around his neck and felt heat radiating from his whole body.

She stroked his head and neck gently as she glanced up at the attendant. "He's burning up," she said. "What's wrong with him?"

The woman looked greatly relieved to see Kirsten. "He became ill shortly after we left Tokyo, and it just kept getting worse. We tried to get him to leave the plane in Hawaii but he refused. Said he'd be all right as soon as he got home, but he nearly collapsed when he stood to get off the plane. I got the wheelchair and took him through customs ahead of the others, but he won't let us send him to a hospital. We were on our way to the first-aid station when he recognized you."

The terror she'd first felt hadn't lessened a bit. She turned her head and nuzzled his burning cheek. "Darling, you've got to see a doctor. Have you any idea what's wrong with you?"

"Yes." His voice was low and raspy. "It's a recurrence of an acute enteritis. I have medication in my luggage. Just take me to one of the airport hotels, and please, stay with me."

"Just try and get rid of me," she whispered, then pushed herself away from him and stood.

He was much too sick to be left sitting there in the airport while she tried to convince him to get medical attention. She'd take him to a hotel and have them send a doctor to his room if she deemed it necessary.

"I'll take responsibility for him," she told the attendant. "I'll get my car and meet you at the curb."

She started to turn away, but the other woman stopped her. "I'll need your name and address. Are you a relative?"

Oh, dear. Kirsten was afraid they wouldn't release him to her if she admitted she wasn't related. Feeling only a slight twinge of conscience, she answered, "I'm his wife."

Court looked up at her with fever-glazed eyes, and with an amused smile reached for her hand and squeezed it.

"May I see some identification, please?" the woman asked.

Kirsten released her hand from Court's and rummaged in her purse for her billfold. She removed her driver's license and handed it over.

The attendant looked at it, then back at Kirsten. "How come you don't have the same last name as your husband?"

"Because I'm his wife, not his mother," Kirsten shot back. "I didn't choose to use his name."

The woman handed the license back and extracted a piece of paper from the briefcase she carried and held it out to Court. "Mr. Forrester, if you'll just sign this release form absolving the airline of all responsibility, you'll be free to leave."

Kirsten wanted to scream with frustration. It seemed as if there were no end to all the red tape, but at last she had Court in her car. He laid his head back against the headrest and closed his eyes as Kirsten guided the vehicle away from the curb. She aimed it for the hotel located at the airport entrance and within seconds drew up in front.

Shutting off the engine, she turned to him and cupped his cheek with her hand. He looked at her. "I love you, Kirsten Anderson," he said softly.

For a moment her heart did cartwheels, but then she realized that it was fever and gratitude talking, not rationality. She leaned over and kissed him. "I'll cherish those words, my darling, but I won't hold you to them. You'd better be a little careful what you say until you're feeling better."

The doorman opened the door on the passenger side, and Court got out. He groaned as he stood, and leaned against the side of the car for support. "I'm sorry. The pounding in my head makes me dizzy."

"I'll get a wheelchair," the doorman said as Kirsten came around the car, but Court stopped him.

"No, that's all right. I can walk. I just need someone to balance me."

He put his arm around Kirsten's shoulder, and she put hers around his waist.

At the front desk Kirsten took charge. "My husband's just landed on a flight from Japan and he's ill," she said briskly. "Could you assign us a room and let me get him settled in bed before we register?"

One look at Court convinced the clerk. "Yes, of course. If you'll just give me your names..." He studied the computer screen.

"Mr. and Mrs. Courtney Forrester," she said, and took the key he handed her.

"We're booked almost solid, and the only rooms I have available are singles with a queen-size bed," he said. "I hope that's satisfactory."

"Fine, thank you." She handed him her car keys. "Our luggage is in the trunk. Please have it sent up right away."

They walked over to the bank of elevators, and one door opened as soon as she pushed the button. Court stood in the corner and leaned back, then put both arms around Kirsten and pulled her full length against him. "I notice you didn't object to a room with only one bed," he whispered in her ear, although there was no one else in the elevator with them.

She cuddled close and was once more alarmed at the heat that emanated from him. "I figure you're in no shape to have your wicked way with me tonight," she teased.

"I'm afraid you're right," he said regretfully. "But tomorrow night..."

"Tomorrow night you'll be home and tucked in your own bed, alone," she told him just as the elevator stopped.

Their room was large with the obligatory picture window and the usual furnishings. Court staggered over to the bed and sat down on the side of it. "Don't lie down until we get your clothes off," Kirsten warned, and knelt in front of him to unbutton his suit coat and unknot his tie.

"I seem to remember we've been through this before," Court said, and there was no levity in his tone.

"Yes." She removed his coat and tie and began unbuttoning his shirt. "And I promised myself it would never happen again. Just shows what a wimp I am." She knew she sounded bitter, but she was.

Court cupped her shoulders. "Kirsten . . ." His voice was ragged with pain and frustration.

"No, Court." She removed his shirt. "We're not going to discuss that now. I know we'll have to later, but not until you're feeling better."

She untied his shoes and pulled them off, then reached for his belt buckle. His hands covered hers and pressed them against his belly. "Sweetheart, I may have a raging fever and be only partially with it, but I can still take off my own pants."

Kirsten felt the warm blush that stole over her, and stood with him as he removed his belt and dropped his trousers.

She kept her gaze above his waist as she helped him lie down and pulled the sheet over him. "Have you been taking aspirin?"

He uttered a sigh of relief as he stretched out on the big bed. "I tried, but they just came up again. I can't keep anything down, not even water."

No wonder his temperature was burning out of control. In the bathroom she filled the ice bucket with lukewarm water and added a washcloth, then set it on the bedside table and bathed Court's overheated face and neck. He sighed. "Mmm, that feels good."

"I'm glad," she murmured as she wrung out the cloth again and laid it across his forehead.

"I'm going down the hall to get a can of 7-Up out of the vending machine. It's easier on your stomach than water and we've got to lower that temperature."

He clasped her hand. "You'll come right back?"

She leaned over and kissed his cheek. "Of course I will. I won't be gone more than a couple of minutes."

The carbonated water and the two aspirin she gave him did go down and gave every indication of staying. Kirsten found a package of straws in the stocked bar in the room and told Court to sip the soda every few minutes while she continued to bathe his face, neck and chest with the luke-warm water.

The bell captain brought Court's luggage and Kirsten found the medication he'd taken for the earlier attack. One was a milky liquid, which she recognized as the prescription strength of a highly effective over-the-counter stomach soother. She poured some into a glass and had him drink it.

The other container was marked One Tablet Four Times A Day, but there were only two tablets left. She didn't want to overtax his traumatized digestive system so she decided to hold off on those and concentrate on getting his temperature under control.

By ten o'clock Court was resting much easier, although he still wasn't asleep. He lay quietly with his eyes open, watching her as she continued to bathe his heated body. She hadn't talked to him because she'd hoped he'd doze, but finally she smiled and said, "Would you think I was taking undue liberties if I sponged off your legs, too?"

He smiled back and reached out one hand to caress the side of her throat. "Honey, nothing would please me more than having your talented little hands running up and down my legs, even if there is a washcloth between your bare skin and mine."

Again she felt the annoying blush spreading across her face, and she got up and took the ice bucket into the bath-room. She refilled it with warm water and grabbed one of the sheet-size bath towels to take back into the bedroom with her.

She put the bucket back on the table and pulled the bed sheet to the bottom of the bed. There was no way she could keep her traitorous gaze away from Court's body stretched out full length, and she noticed that he wore low-cut, royal-blue cotton-knit briefs.

Quickly she covered him from shoulders to thighs with the towel, and dipped the washcloth into the warm, fresh water. Court grinned. "I'm as decently dressed as I would be at the beach," he said wickedly. "There's no need to swathe me like a mummy."

She wouldn't look at him, but attacked his nearest foot with the washcloth. "I don't want you to get a chill."

"Not much chance of that, love," he said as she started up his calf.

She returned to his foot and started over. As she worked she was aware that he had beautifully shaped muscular legs. For that matter, he was gorgeous all over, and in great shape.

He was firm and solid with muscles he didn't get by sitting behind a desk. His abdomen was flat and hard without even a hint of a paunch, and when she finally worked up enough nerve to sponge his thighs, she discovered that they were rugged and strong.

The muscles in them flexed involuntarily, and she quickly decided she'd spent quite enough time on his legs. She pulled the sheet over him again and removed the towel.

"Not quitting already, are you?" he demanded.

"I think you've had enough stimulation," she said with a sniff. "Darn it, Court, you're sick."

He chuckled. "But not as sick as I thought."

Kirsten's face flamed. She knew he was deliberately embarrassing her, but she couldn't control the blush. "In that case you won't miss me if I go down to the desk and register us in."

She started to rise, but he grabbed her hand. "Don't go. I won't tease you anymore. I promise."

She was caught off guard by the apprehension so clearly mirrored on his face. Courtney Forrester was always so in control. She'd never thought of him as actually needing anyone, but now he was reaching out to her. The thought sent a warm feeling of pleasure coursing through her.

She wrapped both her hands around his and brought them to her lips. "I'm only going downstairs," she said between kisses to his fingers. "Remember, I promised I'd go back to check in as soon as I had you settled in bed. I won't be gone more than twenty minutes."

"Yes, I remember," he said, and he sounded very tired. "I don't mean to be so possessive, it's just that . . ."

"Just what?" She held his palm to her cheek.

"Just that when I was sick in Tokyo, and again on the plane, I'd dream that you were there with me. I was so damned grateful, but then when I'd open my eyes you were gone."

"Oh, Court." It was almost a sob as she lowered herself to lie beside him, and he held her close. "I'd never leave you when you needed me."

He turned on his side and tucked her head under his chin. "But how am I going to be sure whether you're real or another figment of my imagination? I seem to drift in and out of reality. If I let you out of my sight, how will I know you'll still be here when I wake up?"

She nuzzled his throat. "Don't worry about it, sweetheart. I'll call down and have them send someone up with whatever papers they want signed. I won't disappear."

Once she and Court were properly registered and she'd given him more aspirin and soda, she took a shower and put on a pair of his pajamas that she found in his luggage. They were maroon cotton and much too big, but she cinched the drawstring waist and rolled up the legs and sleeves.

The light in the bedroom was off, but there was enough illumination from the undraped window to see to get around. Kirsten wasn't used to climbing into bed with a man, and she felt shy and a little wary as she eased herself down beside Court.

She'd hoped he was asleep, but he caught her in his arms and pulled her to him. His hand moved lazily across her back and down the side of her leg, then clenched at the loose cotton fabric. "What on earth have you got on?" he muttered.

She buried her face in his bare chest. "A pair of your pajamas. There are more in your suitcase. Would you like me to get you a pair, too?"

Court laughed and hugged her closer. "Ah, Kirsten, my precious love, you're a constantly shifting delight. You've been bathing my naked body for hours, but still you come to me in bed bundled from chin to toes in swaddling clothes." Once more his hands began to roam. "I can't even find you in all that material."

She was aware that he was no longer radiating such intense heat, and the fact that he could laugh and tease meant he was feeling better. Her relief was great.

She pulled back slightly and raised her hand. "You're not supposed to find me, remember?"

He cuddled her to him again and guided her face back to nestle against his chest. "I remember, sweetheart," he said softly. "You're safe with me tonight. When we finally make love I want to be fully awake and conscious. I don't intend to miss a second of it."

Chapter Eight

Kirsten got up every four hours during the night in order to give Court more aspirin, soda and medicine. Each time, he woke only enough to swallow it down, then once more cradled her against his body and slept.

By seven o'clock in the morning he was much cooler and breathing so easily that she didn't set the alarm again when she crawled back into bed.

She was fully awake at ten, but lay relaxed in the circle of Court's arms. She'd never been so content. It was pure heaven lying in his embrace, their bodies pressed together so intimately and one of his hands cupping her breast.

If she could just wake up this way every morning she'd never ask for another thing, but she wasn't going to delude herself. Instead she'd make the most of it while she could.

She wondered if he would remember much of what happened last night. Probably not. The high temperature and nausea had made him only partially mindful of what was going on. As he'd said, he kept drifting in and out of awareness.

He certainly wouldn't recall telling her he loved her. It was just as well because if he did he'd feel honor bound to act on his declaration. Probably by pretending it was true until he could find a way to let her down easy.

Her stomach rumbled, reminding her that she was ravenous. She'd forgotten all about eating last night. Court would need nourishment, too, but she wasn't going to disturb him again.

Gently she tried to disentangle herself, but he grumbled and clutched her closer. She wanted to stay right where she was, but she knew there'd be no stopping either of them if he woke and found her in his bed.

Finally she managed to ease away and get up. He mumbled sleepily and turned over on his other side.

During the next few hours, while Court slept, Kirsten called Marguerite at work and told her she'd had car trouble in San Francisco the night before and was still there waiting to get it fixed. She couldn't very well tell her supervisor the truth, that she and the big boss had spent the night together.

She'd also had breakfast sent up, and had taken her time eating while reading the morning paper that came with it. At a little after one in the afternoon she was sitting in the lounge chair beside the bed, watching television with the sound turned low when Court spoke to her. "Kirsten, come here."

It was more of an order than a request, and she turned to look at him. The covers had slipped down to slightly below his waist, reminding her that he was nude except for very brief briefs. He smiled and held out one hand. "Come here," he said again, but this time his tone was a caress. "I have to touch you to make sure you're real and not just another dream."

She got up and practically fell on the bed and into his arms. "Oh, yes, you're real all right," he murmured, just before he kissed her.

She accepted his mouth eagerly, and let her hands explore his bare back. He was much cooler than he had been, as well as more vigorous.

"You're all dressed," he said when their lips parted. "What time is it?"

She told him and he groaned. "You should have wakened me, or better yet, stayed in bed." He reached for the buttons of the red-and-cream paisley blouse she wore with her black slacks.

She captured his fingers as they unfastened the first button and started on the second. "Now stop that." Even to her own ears she didn't sound very commanding. "You're sick."

He chuckled, and made quick work of the rest of the obstruction. "Not that sick," he responded, and reached under the blouse to stroke her breast.

It tightened, and seemed to nestle into his palm. "Please, Court," she pleaded in a desperate effort to put a stop to this before her resistance evaporated. "We've got to be sensible."

He sighed and relaxed, but didn't remove his hand. "It's all right, sweetheart. I'm not going to ravage you, but I've missed you so much. I even got a flight out of Tokyo three days earlier than I'd planned because I couldn't stand it any longer. That's why no one met me at the airport last night. I got a last-minute vacancy and didn't have time to make an overseas call to have George meet me with the car."

Kirsten's fingers twisted in the hair on his chest as she mulled over what he was saying. She was delighted to hear that he'd missed her, but if he cared about her at all, then why hadn't he told her he was going on vacation?

Before she could say anything the phone rang, and she turned over to pick it up. She listened, then put her hand over the mouthpiece and looked at Court. "It's the desk. They're reminding us that it's past checkout time, and want to know if we'll be staying another night. Do you feel up to the drive back to San Jose?"

He pushed himself up to a sitting position. "Tell them we'll be checking out in a couple of hours."

She relayed the message as he climbed rather gingerly off the bed. Kirsten caught her breath. She'd never seen him standing up in nothing but briefs before, and the sight was a little overpowering.

He reached out to balance himself with the headboard, and her attention shifted from his physique to his health. "Are you still dizzy?"

"Just a little. I'll be okay as soon as I've had a shower."

Kirsten scrambled off the bed. "While you're doing that I'm going to call room service to send up some soup for you. I had a big breakfast this morning. You won't feel better until you've eaten something."

Two hours later Court sat propped against the headboard of the bed talking on the phone, while Kirsten repacked his two suitcases. He'd dressed in clean brown slacks and a tweed sweater of brown, rust and green, and though he looked and acted much more alert, he was still pale. The large bowl of rich soup had fortified him to some extent, but she noticed that he didn't stand any longer than was necessary.

She shut and locked the last bag as he put down the phone. "They'll have someone up in a few minutes to get the luggage," he said, then patted the side of the bed. "Come over here and let me hold you while we still have some privacy."

She sat down facing him, and he took her in his arms. His sweater was a little rough against her smooth cheek, and she still couldn't identify the scent he wore, but it was masculine and woodsy and stirred her senses almost as much as his touch.

He rubbed his face in her hair. "I wish I could stay here. I suspect that you've put a hex on me, sweetheart. My stomach gets all knotted up again when I think of not having you with me in the same building, the same room, the same bed."

His voice broke, and he took a deep breath. "Do you have to go back to San Jose right away? We could stay here for at least another day or two. I wouldn't keep you cooped up in the hotel room. We can taken in some of the shows. I'm a patron of the opera if you like that type of thing. The city's full of nightclubs we—"

Kirsten reached up and threaded her fingers through the silver in his hair. "Darling, you're forgetting something," she said regretfully. "I'm a working girl. I can't just take off without notice or a good excuse."

He kissed her just below the ear. "Well, I do have some small influence with the head of your company," he said with mock modesty as he nibbled on her lobe. "I'm sure he'd understand if I explained that I need you here with me more than he needs you at the plant."

Kirsten was sorely tempted. Why not spend a few days in this historic old city with Court? It wouldn't hurt anyone, except maybe her, eventually, and she wanted to badly enough to risk almost anything for a little time alone with him. He really did need her, at least until he was well again. He'd proved that.

She'd never felt this closeness with a man before. It was almost as if they were tied together with invisible wires. He knew the words to say, the places to touch, to make her euphoric, and she could anticipate his needs before he even voiced them. As long as they were alone and enclosed in the cocoon of anonymity they were fairy-tale lovers.

A loud rap on the door made her jump, and Court's arms tightened around her so she couldn't pull away. "Kirsten?" His voice was strained. "Shall I send him away? Will you stay with me?"

The bell captain's knock had catapulted her back to reality, and in the real world she and Courtney Forrester weren't fairy-tale lovers at all. They couldn't be more mismatched, and those invisible wires that tied them together weren't wire at all, but threads that could easily be broken when the real world crowded in and separated them.

Her disappointment was so painful that tears pooled in her eyes as she looked at him. "I'm sorry, Court. Every nerve in my body screams at me to ignore the barriers and give in to my desire for you. I want you so much, but there are already too many problems between us. If we made love it would only create more."

He didn't attempt to disguise the pain that twisted his features, but as the knock sounded again he lowered his head and took her mouth in a hard, stinging kiss, then deepened it until her head swirled and her body tingled.

It was the third, louder knock that finally separated them, and Kirsten slid off the bed and walked to the door.

Twenty minutes later they'd checked out of the hotel, and Kirsten was driving south on Highway 101. Court had adjusted the back of the passenger seat and it reclined at a comfortable angle. Dark glasses protected his sensitized eyes from the afternoon sun, and he still looked tired and pale. Impulsively she reached over and put her hand on his thigh. "You don't feel very well yet, do you?"

He covered her hand with his and held it there. "I'm fine, sweetheart. How could I not be, with you taking care of me? I can't tell you how much it meant to me to find you in that crowded airport. If I didn't believe in miracles before, I do now. Incidentally, you didn't say what you were doing there."

"I'd driven Dad over to catch a plane for Washington, D.C. His flight had just left and I was on my way back to the car when your stewardess caught up with me. I'm just thankful that you recognized me in that crush of people."

He rubbed her hand against his leg. "It's odd," he said thoughtfully. "I was being pushed along and all of a sudden I had this...this compulsion...to look up. My head hurt so badly that the last thing I wanted was to move it, but I couldn't fight the strong urgency to do so. All I saw was your back striding away from me, but I never doubted that it was you. I yelled your name and told the attendant to catch you."

He picked up her hand and carried it to his lips. "No one will ever convince me that you weren't destined to be in that place at that time to rescue me." He kissed the back of her hand, then turned it over and kissed the palm. "I'd never have made it through the night without you. Others can call it coincidence, but it will always be a miracle to me."

She glanced at him without taking her full attention away from the road in front of her. He sounded so sincere. It would be easy to believe that he really had missed her and wanted to be with her if only...

She'd never been one to speculate if it were possible to get the facts. This subject had to be dealt with soon, so it might as well be now. Gently she pulled her hand away from him and put it back on the steering wheel. "Court, why didn't you tell me you were leaving on vacation?"

He stiffened and sat up straighter. "Vacation? What made you think I was on vacation?"

Kirsten blinked with surprise. "Noelle told me you were."

"Noelle?" He looked at her as if she were speaking gibberish. "When did you talk to Noelle?"

"It was on Saturday after we'd quarreled," she explained. "I was desperate to explain that you'd misunderstood what I'd said, and I tried to call you at the office, but Tanya would only say you weren't available. Since I didn't have your unlisted home phone, I decided on Saturday to go to the estate and try to talk to you in person."

Court seemed to relax a little, and once more settled back in the reclining seat as she continued. "The security guard said you weren't 'in residence' and wouldn't let me through the gate, but just then Noelle drove up. She asked what I wanted, and when I told her I needed to talk to you she said you were on vacation."

Court sighed. "I'm sorry, honey, but you must have misunderstood Noelle. I haven't been on vacation. I've been in the Orient on business. I got a call the morning after we'd had dinner to alert me that the business conference I'd requested had been arranged for early the following Monday morning in Tokyo. By the time I made travel arrangements, got all my data together and talked to the people I had to confer with here, I made it to the first meeting with only a few hours to spare."

Kirsten was glad that it had been an emergency business meeting and not a long-planned vacation that had taken him out of the country, but her joy was overshadowed by his casual assumption that she'd misunderstood his daughter. It didn't once occur to him that Noelle might have deliberately lied to her in order to cause trouble.

If one of them was in the wrong it obviously had to be Kirsten.

They rode along in silence for a few minutes, then Court spoke again. "I'm sorry you weren't able to get in touch with me. That's one of the problems of being hemmed in by security. If you'll remind me when we get home, I'll write my unlisted number down for you."

She shrugged, discouraged. "That's not necessary. I probably won't need to get in touch with you again outside of office hours."

He looked at her and frowned. "Of course you will. I want you to call me. I should have let you know I was leaving but we'd quarreled and, frankly, I was still mad as hell. I figured it would be better not to talk to you again until I'd had a chance to cool off."

"And are you cooled off now?" She knew she sounded waspish, but she was hurt.

He touched his hand to his forehead, and she knew the headache was back again. "I learned that it didn't matter," he said wearily. "I wanted you no matter what your reasons were for submitting."

She winced at the sharpness of the pain that slashed through her. "Well, thanks a lot," she said sarcastically. "It's nice to know you have such a high regard for me."

Court took off his dark glasses and rubbed his eyes. "Dammit, Kirsten," he said angrily, "what was I supposed to think? I'd just told you that your pet project wasn't economically feasible, and then after we'd started making love and I was almost past rational thought, you asked if I'd reconsider."

He put his glasses in his jacket. "There's something you should know about me if you're still hell-bent on that daycare center. I don't like being used."

He settled back in the seat and turned his head away.

That was just as well because she didn't want him to see the tears that blurred her vision and spilled over to trickle down her cheeks. At the next exit she turned off the highway. Court opened his eyes and looked around. "Where are you going?" he asked, puzzled.

"To find a service station." She kept her face averted.

"But you have almost a full tank of gas..."

She sniffled, and in spite of pinching her lips together a sob escaped.

He sat up straight. "Kirsten, are you crying?"

He cupped her chin with his hand and tried to turn her head toward him, but she shook him off. Too late; his palm was wet with her tears.

"Oh, sweetheart, don't cry." It was a heartfelt plea. "I'm sorry. I was hurt and angry, but I didn't mean to upset you so." He caressed her thigh.

She drove into the gas station at the end of the exit ramp and stopped. Without saying anything to Court she got out of the car and hurried into the rest room where the sobs she'd dammed up shook her with their release.

For a long time she sat on the closed lid of the commode and let the tears and the sobs come. Damn Court for making her cry. She hadn't wept since her dog was run over and killed when she was in junior high school. The women of the eighties didn't weep. They didn't have time. They were too busy changing the world single-handedly.

She'd left her purse in the car so she used toilet paper to blow her nose and mop at her streaming eyes. Was that what she was trying to do? Change the workplace all by herself in a matter of weeks? Was she expecting more from Court than was reasonable?

On a rational level she couldn't blame him for thinking she was using him. After her blunder that night in her apartment, he'd have had to be a mind reader not to misunderstand, but her love for him wasn't rational. It involved deep and interrelated emotions that were lacerated by the fact that he'd actually thought she was capable of being so calculating and deceitful.

Was she looking for a knight in shining armor instead of a flesh-and-blood man? Would he believe her when she finally got the chance to explain, or was he using her supposed deviousness as an excuse to make love to her without committing himself to a stronger, more lasting relationship?

A knock on the door distracted her. "Kirsten, are you all right?"

It was Court, but she couldn't pull herself together enough to answer.

A few minutes later he knocked again, louder this time. "Kirsten, please, come out of there."

She made an effort to control the sobs that still buffeted her as she tore off more bathroom tissue and blew her nose. She couldn't talk to him yet; he'd just have to wait.

The next time he pounded with his fists and shouted, "Kirsten, if you don't open the door right now, I'm going to get the key and come in after you."

It wasn't anger but concern in his tone, and she knew she couldn't ignore it this time. Taking a deep breath, she hoped her voice would sound reasonably steady. "I'm fine, and I'll be out in a minute," she called. "Please, just go back to the car and wait for me."

"Honey, I—"

"Darn it, Court, leave me alone," she snapped, and got up to turn on the faucet in the sink.

She splashed her face with warm water, but without makeup there was nothing she could do to hide the ravages her childish crying jag had caused. Her eyes were red and swollen, and her face was white with a pink, raw-looking path down each cheek where the tears had streamed. Her lips were devoid of color, and her hair was tousled from running her hands through it.

She looked awful. She always did when she cried. Well, there was nothing she could do about it now. She didn't even have a comb.

It didn't matter how she looked anyway. She'd get back in the car and explain to Court as best she could why she'd seemed to be exchanging her favors for the day-care center just before he'd left for the Orient. She doubted that he'd believe her, but again it didn't matter. He'd as much as told her it was only her body he wanted, anyway.

She retied the bow at the neck of her blouse and adjusted the suit coat that matched her slacks. It was only a few more miles to San Jose. She'd leave Court to the tender mercies of Mrs. Underhill, and tomorrow she'd start tying up loose ends at work so the transition would be smooth when she left Evergreen Industries in three and a half weeks.

That thought wrung another sob from her aching chest.

Court was waiting just outside the restroom door, and she almost ran into him. He reached for her, but she quickly sidestepped and walked stiffly ahead of him to the car.

Slipping in behind the wheel, she started the engine while he walked around and got in on the passenger side. "Why don't you let me drive the rest of the way?" he asked softly.

She shifted gears and eased the vehicle out into the street. "I prefer to drive my own car," she said, and made a U-turn at the intersection.

Court sat hunched in his seat, looking thoroughly miserable. "Kirsten, I'm sorry. I—"

"No, Court," she interrupted, "I'm the one who's sorry. As you pointed out, you don't have anything to apologize for."

"That's not what I—"

"Please, let me finish." She'd finally regained control of her voice and her composure, and she intended to get this matter cleared up, now.

"My behavior the night you came to dinner at my apartment was incredibly naive and offensive, but I truly didn't intend it that way. You'd requested a business meal, and in my zeal to please you I inadvertently set up a seduction."

He looked as if he were going to interrupt and she plunged ahead. "I did all the wrong things, from preparing an intimate candlelit gourmet meal to wearing a sexy outfit that was totally inappropriate."

This time he did interrupt. "You looked like a mischievous imp in those slinky purple pajamas," he said, his tone reminiscent. "I'd hoped you'd worn them just for me."

She hesitated, shaken by his tenderness. "I did. That's what I'm trying to tell you. I wanted you to know the basic me, without the tailored suits, the sensible shoes and the subdued makeup and jewelry. I wanted to show you that there's more to me than just the efficient career woman; that I'm also sexy, and domestic, and loving..."

He put his hand on her knee. "Honey, I've always known that. It shines right through the suits and sensible shoes, even while you're badgering me about day-care centers. If you were any more sexy and loving I'd carry you off to a cave somewhere and never let you go."

"Day-care centers, again," she said bitterly. "I wish I'd never heard of them. This is the last time I'll take up the banner for someone else's cause. It's brought me nothing but grief, and it's not even something I'd benefit from."

"Don't you plan on having children?" he asked quietly.

"Sure I do, but you were right about me from the beginning. I'd never allow anyone else to raise them. I don't have to. I have enough money of my own from trust funds and investments to live comfortably even without working. So, you see, I'm really not dedicated enough to the cause to sell myself body and soul to you or anyone else just to get it implemented."

Court frowned and removed his hand from her leg. "Kirsten..."

She continued as though he hadn't spoken. "Actually, it was a good old-fashioned case of bridal panic that tripped me up that night, only I wasn't a bride. I hadn't expected things to proceed as far or as fast as they did, and I was having second thoughts. You know, wondering if you'd still respect me in the morning, that sort of thing.''

He was staring at her. ''Good Lord, you can't be serious—''

''Why not? Did you think I went to bed with every man I cooked dinner for? Also, you weren't just any man, you were my boss, and you'd made it plain that you had no intention of getting involved with me. I wasn't suitable. I was too young, I was an employee, you had grown children who would object and I'd never measure up to your wife—''

All of a sudden the traffic in front of her slowed. She slammed on the brakes, throwing them both against their seat belts, and they stopped just inches away from the car in front of them.

''Dammit, Kirsten,'' he grated. ''Either slow down and watch where you're going or let me drive.'' He leaned back against the reclining seat and closed his eyes.

She was shivering with reaction as she took her foot off the brake and let the Jaguar move ahead at the slower pace. He was right; she'd been driving too fast and hadn't been paying close enough attention to the traffic.

She put on her turn signal to change lanes. ''I'm sorry. I guess I am too upset to drive. I'll turn off at the next exit and let you take over.''

The next exit was the one she would have taken anyway to get to Court's estate, and once they were off it she pulled over to the side of the street and stopped. They both got out and met in front of the car, and this time he caught and held her. She was too shaky to pull away, and allowed herself to be cradled against him.

''You're trembling,'' he murmured. ''Oh, sweetheart, I'm so sorry...''

She shook her head against his chest. ''It's just a reaction to the near accident. That wasn't your fault.''

Gathering all her wavering strength, she pushed herself back and stepped away from him. "We'd better be on our way. Are you sure you feel up to driving?"

Reluctantly, he let her go. "I'm afraid I'm in better shape than you are right now. We'll leave, but when we get home you're going to listen to what I have to say."

They got back into the car, and he started the engine and eased onto the street.

Kirsten leaned back and took deep breaths in an effort to stop the shivering. Court was right; she was in bad shape. She must have been under more stress during the time he was gone than she'd realized. Well, that was even more reason for her to complete her apology...explanation...whatever, and get away from him before she fell apart completely.

She twisted her hands together on her lap. "To get on with what I was saying—"

"It can wait until we get home," he interrupted.

"No, it can't. I've been agonizing about this for weeks, and now I'm going to get it over with. You're an expert lover, and when I realized that either I had to stop you immediately or not at all, I started casting around in my mind for a way to cool things down a little. The only subject I could come up with was the one we'd just been discussing, the day-care issue. I simply said the first thing that came to mind. I didn't plan it or have any ulterior motive, I just spoke without thinking."

She cleared her throat in an effort to stop another sob. "How could I think when you were driving me crazy with your hands, and your lips, and your unspoken but very obvious need?"

She covered her face with her hands and cursed the tears that once more flowed down her ravaged cheeks.

The car swerved and screeched to a halt as Kirsten's head snapped up. Before she could get her bearings, Court had slammed the door on his side and was opening the one next to her.

He reached in and practically lifted her out and into his arms. "Talk about being driven crazy," he muttered huskily. "That's exactly what you've been doing to me for weeks now."

He caught her lower lip between his teeth and nibbled tenderly as he teased her mouth open, then covered it with his own. His tongue stroked hers, then allowed hers to take over and return the pleasure. Her fingers caressed the back of his neck while his hands sought to memorize every curve and crevice of her back and hips.

She was vaguely aware that it was nearly dark, and they were on the private road that led to the Forrester estate, but it wouldn't have made any difference if they'd stopped on the freeway in broad daylight. Nothing mattered but the two of them, and the relief that overrode any negative emotion when Court held her and kissed her.

This man was dangerous. He had a power over her that even her parents had never had. With a touch, a kiss and a few passionate words he could coax her to do anything he wanted. She knew it but she didn't care, and that was the most frightening thing of all.

He moved his lips to her throat, and she held her head back to expose as much as possible to his attention. He handled her so gently, but she could sense the smoldering passion that he kept leashed. What would it be like if he were to let go and make love to her with the full force of that ardor?

The very thought made her tremble, and it was then that she realized he was trembling, too. "I'm going to take you home with me," he said between nibbles at sensitive spots that sent her blood racing. "And we're going to curl up together and talk about all the things that bother us. Get all our problems out in the open where we can deal with them."

He looked at her and smiled. "I'm too damn old to have my emotions stirred up to such a high pitch all the time. It's great when we're making out, but it's hell when we quarrel."

Kirsten sniffled and smiled back. "You've just put your finger on one of our problems—your obsession with age." Her smile broadened to a teasing grin. "I absolutely guarantee that if you get involved with me I'll keep your hormones so churned up that you'll never get any older."

Court laughed with unrestrained glee and swatted her playfully on the bottom. "Careful, young lady. Don't make promises you don't intend to keep, because I'm going to hold you to that one. Now get in the car and let's go home."

Ten minutes later they'd cleared with the guard at the gate, and Court stopped the Jaguar in the wide, lighted driveway next to a familiar white BMW convertible. He frowned. "Looks like Noelle is here," he said without much enthusiasm.

Kirsten's disappointment was laced with apprehension. The last person she wanted to confront right now was Court's daughter. How could she have forgotten that Noelle always came first with him?

They got out of the car and she was walking slightly behind him up the sidewalk when the front door opened and Noelle came running out. "Daddy," she squealed, and threw herself into Court's arms. "Bud just called to say you were on your way. We weren't expecting you till tomorrow."

Court hugged her and kissed her on the cheek. "Hello, baby. I got lonesome so I came back early. Have you been behaving yourself while I was gone?"

Kirsten stepped back and waited while Noelle put her arm through Court's and started to lead him the rest of the way up the sidewalk, but he balked. "Hey, wait for Kirsten."

He partially turned and held his other arm out to her while still talking to Noelle. "She was kind enough to give me a ride home from San Francisco."

He caught Kirsten's hand and drew her forward until he could put his arm around her waist.

Noelle obviously hadn't seen Kirsten in the darkening shadows, and she glared at her with surprise and disapproval. "So you finally caught up with him," she said angrily. "How did you know he was flying in early? Nobody else did."

"That's enough, Noelle," he snapped. "Kirsten didn't know I was flying into San Francisco. She was there seeing her father off on another flight and we just happened to run into each other."

"Oh, come on, Dad. Just *happened* to run into each other? That's a little too much of a coincidence even for Kirsten." There was venom in her tone. "Did she tell you that she threatened to hit me when she came here while you were gone?"

Chapter Nine

Kirsten felt rather than heard Court's sharp intake of breath, and his fingers dug into the side of her waist.

She should have expected a low blow like that from Noelle Forrester, but she hadn't. It stunned her and made the muscles in her stomach clench painfully.

Court looked from Noelle to Kirsten, then paused as if waiting for something. When neither woman spoke he turned his full attention to Kirsten. "Aren't you going to deny it?"

She was strongly tempted to do just that and accuse Noelle of lying. She couldn't prove her accusation. It was just her word against Kirsten's.

Fortunately her innate sense of honor overcame her weakness, and she shook her head slowly. "No, I'm not going to deny it. It's true. I did threaten to slap her."

The pain and disappointment that settled on Court's face was like a knife twisting in her chest, and she found it difficult to breathe.

A quick glance at Noelle revealed the younger woman's surprise and chagrin. It was only then that Kirsten realized Court's daughter had hoped to trap her into lying, secure in the knowledge that her father would have believed her instead of Kirsten.

When he spoke again Court sounded sick, and not just physically. "Come in the house. Obviously we need to talk."

He pulled away from Noelle and dropped his arm from around Kirsten's waist, then stood back and let them precede him.

Much to her annoyance, Kirsten felt exactly the way she'd felt as a teenager those times when she and her sister Ingrid had quarreled, and their father had marched them into his den, for one of his "you two are behaving like a couple of alley cats" lectures.

It was the first time she'd ever thought of Court as a father figure, and the idea was repulsive to her.

"We'll discuss this in the den," he said, his tone crisp and angry, and Kirsten almost groaned. He sounded exactly like Dane had, but Kirsten wasn't Court's daughter. She didn't have to stay and let him discipline her.

He had the right to an explanation, though, and she wasn't going to leave without defending herself against Noelle's blunt accusation.

The den was a wood-paneled room with a fireplace, built-in cabinets and leather furnishings. There was also a large desk with an Evergreen personal computer at one end and stacks of papers and file folders scattered across the rest of it.

Definitely a male-oriented hideaway, and the only room she'd seen so far in this house that didn't have at least one glass wall.

The two lamps were lit, and Court also turned on the ceiling fixture above the desk. It was then that Kirsten noticed the picture that hung over the fireplace mantel. It was a large oil painting of a slender blond woman wearing a flowing pink dress. She was seated on a white wrought-iron bench amid a profusion of flowering camellias. Her resemblance to Noelle was unmistakable.

"That's my mother," Noelle said, apparently having noticed Kirsten's interest in the picture. "She had it painted as a gift for Dad on their fifteenth wedding anniversary. There were tears in his eyes when he unwrapped it, and I'll never forget what he said to her."

"Noelle!" Court roared, but she didn't skip a beat.

"He said, 'I'll treasure it, but I don't need a picture. You're always with me, in my mind and in my heart.'"

Kirsten reeled, and wrapped her arms around herself in an effort to ward off the anguish that buffeted her. If Noelle was looking for a way to get back at her, she'd found it with a vengeance. The blow she'd just delivered had landed straight and true.

In a fog she heard Court berating his daughter, but her first impulse was to get away from there. She did turn, but something stopped her. If she walked out now, she could forget about a future with him. After weeks of insisting she could handle the numerous problems he considered insurmountable, she couldn't go to pieces the first time she was challenged.

She focused her attention on Court's and Noelle's angry words, and heard him saying, "My feelings for your mother were private, personal and not a subject to be discussed by you or any other member of the family. I'm ashamed of you, Noelle. You're behaving like a spoiled child."

Noelle looked stricken. "I'm sorry, Daddy. I just wanted Kirsten to know that she can never take Mama's place."

Court's shoulders slumped, and for a moment he seemed unable, or unwilling, to comment.

Kirsten straightened, silently cursing Noelle's insensitivity. She might have been willing to tear her father apart in order to make her point, but Kirsten wasn't.

"Noelle was just making sure I knew that you loved her mother very dearly," she said, and was pleased that her agitation didn't sound in her voice. "I was already aware of that, and it's one of the reasons I respect you so much, but I can't blame her for wanting to protect her mother's memory."

She focused her attention on Noelle. "Now, to get back to the subject of our little cat fight. Aren't you going to tell your father why I threatened to slap you?"

Noelle's mouth dropped open in surprise, and Kirsten realized that Noelle hadn't expected her to defend herself. Apparently she hadn't thought past the bombshell of her accusation.

"Well, Noelle?" Court said. "I assume she didn't just walk up and threaten to hit you for no reason. Suppose you tell me what led up to this." His tone was dangerously calm.

"I—I, well, that is, she . . . she misunderstood something I said," Noelle stammered.

"I didn't misunderstand a thing," Kirsten replied firmly. "After she told me you were on vacation she invited me up here for a drink. When I admitted that I didn't know the layout of the house she asked if you'd rushed me right upstairs to bed the other time I was here without giving me a tour of the premises."

The look on his face was cold and furious as he turned to his daughter. Noelle shrank back. "No, it wasn't like that," she said quickly. "She misunderstood. I was only teasing."

"Teasing?" He sounded drained, ill, and Kirsten suspected that the enteritis was back in full force. "I sincerely hope not. If you were, it indicates a cruel, perverted sense of humor. I'm not surprised Kirsten threatened you."

Noelle sank down in one of the soft leather chairs and started to cry. Court watched her for a moment, then walked over to the fireplace, folded his arms on the mantel and buried his face in them.

Kirsten knew it was time for her to leave, but first she had to talk to Noelle. She walked over to stand in front of the stricken young woman who was sobbing like a broken-hearted child. "Noelle, listen to me, please. I have something to tell you."

Noelle dug at her red eyes with the back of her fists and looked up at Kirsten.

"Your father is ill," she said, not wanting to alarm her. "It's something he picked up in the Orient."

Noelle's eyes widened. "Dad's sick?" She looked at her father, then stood up. "Why didn't you tell me?"

"You really didn't give us much chance, did you? You didn't even ask him how he was after being gone for so long, but started right in, trying to discredit me."

Another sob shook Noelle, and Kirsten put her hand on the younger woman's arm. "I'm sorry. I don't want to make you feel even worse, but I'm not going to be blamed for something that wasn't my fault. Let's try to get along for the next few minutes and not cause Court any more grief than we already have."

She took her hand from Noelle's arm. "He saw the doctor in Tokyo, but he's out of the medication that I suspect was the most important. He needs to see his own doctor. Does he have one who will make house calls?"

Noelle nodded. "Yes." She started to walk toward the desk, but Kirsten stopped her.

"I assume there's a phone in the kitchen. Could you use it, and then bring him a glass of ginger ale when you come back?"

Noelle changed direction. "Sure..." Again she glanced at Court. "Shouldn't he be in bed?"

"He never should have gotten out of bed in the first place," Kirsten said.

Noelle left, and Kirsten went to stand beside Court. She reached out and gently massaged the back of his neck. He raised his head and turned to take her in his arms. "I don't need a doctor," he said against her hair, "just a little peace of mind."

She put her arms around his waist. He was radiating heat again, and she knew he felt miserable.

"You need both," she said, "and in a few minutes you'll get them. I'll leave as soon as I know the doctor's coming, then things should settle down around here."

He hugged her close. "No. Don't go away. Stay with me. I'll send Noelle back to the sorority house."

Kirsten was childishly pleased to know that he wanted her with him instead of his daughter, then hated herself for being so petty. "No, darling, that would only make things worse. She's already been seared by your displeasure. Don't send her away, too. She needs time to get used to the idea that you might someday fall in love again."

"Someday's already come, and she'd better not take too long to accept it. I'm not a patient man. Please change your mind." His voice dropped to a husky whisper. "I need you sweetheart."

When he talked like that she'd do anything he wanted, but this time she had to bolster her wavering resolve and get out of there.

"I'm sorry now that we didn't stay in San Francisco." She put her hand under his sweater and caressed the firm muscles of his back. "I'd love to be with you tonight, but since Noelle feels the way she does, it would only make things worse. Will you call me tomorrow evening and let me know how you are?"

He swayed slightly with the rhythm of her fingers. "If you promise to keep that up I'll go home with you right now," he murmured, just as Noelle came soundlessly through the door.

Kirsten quickly took her hands from under his sweater and tried to pull away from him, but his hold on her tightened for a moment before he let her go.

"Thank you, honey," he said to his daughter as she handed him a glass of sparkling soda without comment. The look on her face made her disapproval plain enough, but his nonchalant stance warned her that she'd better keep it to herself.

Kirsten picked up her purse. "Is the doctor coming?" she asked, and was relieved that she sounded calm.

"He said he'd be here in twenty minutes." Noelle looked at Court. "He wants you to go to bed but not to take anything, not even aspirin, until he's examined you. I'll get George to help you upstairs."

"I don't need help," Court said impatiently, then apparently realized he'd been waspish and reached out to her. "I'm all right, Noelle," He drew her close. "All I really need is some rest. It's been an exhausting couple of weeks. Try to overlook my short temper until I get my bearings again, okay?"

Kirsten opened her purse, then remembered she didn't have her keys. "I'll be going now," she said. "Do you have my keys, Court?"

"I left them in your car." He came toward her. "George needed them to get my bags from the trunk. I'll walk out with you." He took her arm.

"Oh, that's not necessary," she protested as he ushered her into the hall. "You'd better go to bed."

He put his arm around her waist and hugged her against his side. "I'd be a lot more anxious to go to bed if you'd come with me."

"Please don't tempt me," she begged. "I don't know how much longer I can resist."

They'd reached the front door, and he turned and took her in his arms. "If I thought there was any chance you'd change your mind I'd pick you up and carry you off to the bedroom."

She put her arms around his neck, reluctant to leave him. "You will call me tomorrow, won't you?"

He kissed the tip of her nose. "Sweetheart, I'll come to your house and give you a report in person." Reaching out behind her, he opened the door.

"Please don't come outside," she said anxiously. "It's damp and chilly and you're burning with fever."

"All right," he answered reluctantly, and pushed one of a panel of buttons on the wall beside them. "I'm not going to kiss you. The damage is probably already done, but when we kissed earlier I didn't realize I was so sick."

They were still gazing into each other's eyes when the employee named George appeared. "You rang, sir?"

Court released her and stepped back. "Yes. Please see that Ms. Anderson gets to her car safely. You did get my luggage out of it, didn't you?"

"Yes, sir, I did." He opened the door wide for Kirsten. "After you, Miss."

She walked out into the cold night air and tried to brush aside the strong suspicion that she was making a big mistake by leaving.

Kirsten had hardly gotten her coat off the next morning, Tuesday, before she was called into Marguerite's office. The attractive dark-haired personnel manager was sitting at her desk, her brown eyes scanning a sheet of stationery that Kirsten recognized as containing her resignation.

"What is this nonsense?" Marguerite asked as Kirsten closed the door behind her.

"It's not nonsense. I'll be leaving the middle of December, but I'll be happy to train my successor..."

"We won't even discuss such an eventuality," the manager snapped. "What is it you want? More money? Less responsibility? Better working conditions?"

Kirsten sighed and sat down. "Oh Margie, it's not any of those things. I just feel that it's time for me to move on..."

"What about the day-care center you've been so passionately pursuing? Are you just going to walk away from it?" Marguerite's brown eyes flashed with anger.

Kirsten shook her head. "I'm afraid that's a lost cause. Mr. Forrester seems adamant about not getting involved in his employees' babysitting problems."

"Is that why you're leaving?"

"Not really. I mean it's not that I'm walking out because I can't have my own way, but I feel as if I've botched the whole project. Maybe later someone else can bring it up again and have better luck."

"I don't buy that for a minute," Marguerite snapped, and for the next half hour Kirsten was forced to defend her decision to resign while being careful not to mention her personal relationship with the head of the company.

The rest of the day she spent trying to catch up after having been gone the day before. Even so, in the back of her mind was a nagging worry about Court. How was he? What had the doctor said? What further deviltry was Noelle plotting?

On the stroke of five she left work and hurried home. She'd asked Court to call, and he'd said he'd come over. She prepared for both eventualities by changing into a clinging blue silk dress, then quickly eating a TV dinner while sitting beside the telephone.

It rang but it was a charity solicitor. Fifteen minutes later one of the men she'd been dating called to ask if she'd like to take in a movie. Shortly after she got rid of him her mother called.

By ten o'clock Kirsten was pacing the floor. Why didn't Court contact her? He'd promised that he would. He must have known how worried she'd be about him. Was this some more of Noelle's doing?

By eleven, Kirsten was nearly frantic. Was it possible that he'd contracted some rare exotic illness in the Orient? Maybe he'd been taken to a hospital! She would have called him, but with all the uproar Noelle had caused when they got to his place yesterday, he'd forgotten to give her his private number, and she hadn't thought to remind him.

At midnight, torn between fear and anger, she undressed and went to bed, but sleep eluded her. She tossed and turned and finally dozed off about an hour before the alarm wakened her again. Tumbling out of bed, she hoped a long, stinging shower would make her feel reasonably human.

The phone was ringing when she came out of the bathroom. Her taut nerves screamed as the bell shattered the quiet, and she stumbled and fell across the bed in her dash to pick it up.

"Good morning, sweetheart," said Court's baritone voice from the other end. "Did I wake you?"

If she'd had him in the room with her she'd have strangled him with the telephone cord. "No, you didn't waken me," she snapped. "Dammit, Court, why didn't you call last night. I've been frantic—"

"I'm sorry," he said, and truly sounded contrite. "I'd planned to phone you at seven, but Mrs. Underhill insisted that I take my medicine after I'd had a bowl of soup, and obviously one of the pills was a sedative. It knocked me out and I just surfaced a few minutes ago."

Kirsten felt weak with relief. "Thank heaven you're all right. I've been so worried."

"Why didn't you call me? At least you could have talked to Mrs. Underhill or Noelle and found out that I was just sleeping."

"I don't have your unlisted number, remember?"

Court muttered an oath. "Get a paper and pencil and I'll give it to you right now before I forget again."

"I don't need to write it down, I'll remember." As if she could ever forget it!

He recited it for her, and she consigned it to memory.

"Now," she said, "tell me what the doctor found wrong with you?"

"He just confirmed the Japanese doctor's diagnosis. It's a parasite that takes a little while to deal with. I'm feeling much better this morning, and since today's the last working day until after the Thanksgiving vacation, I'll have until Monday to recover."

Kirsten had almost forgotten. "That's right, tomorrow's Thanksgiving."

"Right, and my son, John, is flying in from New Haven tonight to spend the holiday with Noelle and me. I want you to meet him, Kirsten."

The idea of meeting Court's son terrified her. If he was anything like Court's daughter, Kirsten didn't think she was up to it. Noelle was about all any sane person could handle. "Oh, Court, I don't think—"

"You've got to meet him someday." Court's tone told her he wasn't going to accept any excuses. "And I want it to be now. You'll like him. He's a great kid."

A nineteen-year-old was no "kid" in Kirsten's point of view, and she'd bet her car that he wasn't going to be any more enthusiastic about her...um...friendship...with his father than his sister was.

"I'm sure I will, darling, but—"

Court interrupted before she could think of an excuse, which he probably wouldn't have accepted anyway. "Are you free to come to dinner on Friday? Is six okay? Both Johnny and Noelle have plans for the afternoon, but they'll be here by seven."

Both of them? Good grief, she was going to have to face both of his adult children at the same time!

Oh, what the hell. She might as well do it and get it over with. At least then she'd know what she was up against.

Kirsten spent Thanksgiving Day with her family, which included grandparents, aunts, uncles and cousins. There were twenty-three around the huge dining-room table, and for most of the time she managed to forget her upcoming dinner with the Forrester family and enjoy herself.

Ingrid's infant daughter was a special delight, and Kirsten snatched every opportunity to hold her, rock her and play little laughing games with her. Although she tried not to think about it, she knew that her strong desire for babies of her own could be another stumbling block with Court. Would he be willing to start another family now that his first one was grown?

She chided herself for building roadblocks where there wasn't even a road. Court had only told her he loved her once, and that was when he was half-delirious. The word marriage had never been mentioned. If he wanted her at all it was probably as a temporary mistress, and that was one role Kirsten would never play.

Not even for a man she loved as much as she loved Court.

On Friday morning Kirsten slept late, and when she got up she dressed in faded jeans and an old sweatshirt that was soft and comfortable with dozens of washings.

She'd just finished making her bed when the doorbell rang. With a glance in the mirror and a grimace at her shiny face free of makeup and her tangled hair held back with a colorful scarf twisted around her head, she ran down the stairs as the bell rang again.

She wasn't expecting anyone, and hoped it wasn't somebody with impromptu plans for the day. She intended to spend hours on her hair, her makeup and her clothes before meeting Court's son that evening. She wanted to look just right, not necessarily older but still mature and sophisticated.

She opened the door just as the bell rang for the third time. Standing on the other side of the screen was a tall, dark-haired man dressed in jeans and a heavy gray-and-silver pullover sweater. He was probably in his early twenties, and although his expression was solemn his features were marvelously symmetrical. Handsome enough to be one of those male models on the "hunk of the month" calendars so popular with high school and college girls. Kirsten wondered what he was doing on her doorstep.

She smiled, and he looked her over, then smiled back. "Hi," he said. "Is this the Anderson residence?"

"Yes, it is."

"I'm John Forrester, and I'd like to talk to Kirsten Anderson."

Court's son. Oh no! He'd caught her looking like the cleaning lady!

For a moment she was too startled to do anything but continue smiling as she unlocked the screen and stood back to let him in. She knew she should say something, but her brain seemed to be scrambled. Why had John Forrester come to see her? He was alone, so Court hadn't brought him.

He regarded her with amused tolerance as they stood silently in the hallway. "Is your mother here?" he asked after a moment.

She blinked. "My... my mother?"

Now he looked confused. "I'm sorry. I thought maybe you were Ms. Anderson's daughter."

Daughter! Good grief, hadn't anyone told him her age? The picture of herself that she'd seen in the mirror just minutes before flashed through her mind. Scruffy jeans, tacky sweatshirt, limp hair and no makeup. She probably did look like a teenager.

Kirsten almost groaned aloud. So much for her "maturely sophisticated" image. But even so...

With a concentrated effort she managed to get her expression under control and her shoulders pulled back in a more dignified stance. "I'm sorry, but you took me by surprise." She even managed another smile. "*I'm* Kirsten. Please, won't you come in?"

She started to turn toward the living room, but this time it was John who was dumbfounded. His mouth dropped open and he stared. "*You're* Kirsten?" His tone was a mixture of disbelief and outrage. "There must be some mistake. You aren't any older than I am!"

A chill of apprehension made her shiver. Obviously Johnny wasn't going to be any more tolerant of her relationship with his father than his sister was. Could Noelle have deliberately misled him, letting him think Kirsten was nearer Court's age just so the truth would be that much more upsetting to him?

Yes, of course she could, and probably did. Noelle was apparently intent on using any means at her disposal to keep her father from becoming further involved with Kirsten.

"I'm twenty-five," she said quietly, "and I'm very much in love with your father. Now please come in the living room and sit down where we can be comfortable. It looks like this discussion will go on for some time."

When they were settled—he in the big chair, while she curled up at one end of the sofa—Kirsten spoke first. "Why did you come here, Johnny? It can't have been just to meet me since I'll be having dinner at your house tonight."

He seemed discomfited by her bluntness. "Well, no, it wasn't. That is, I wanted to talk to you alone without Dad present."

"I see." Kirsten wasn't nearly as calm as she sounded. "What do you want to talk about? It can't be the difference in Court's and my ages since you apparently didn't know about it until you saw me."

He shifted in the chair. "Uh, no, I didn't, but that's all the more reason... I mean..." He took a deep breath and blurted out, "What is it you want from Dad? You can't be in love with him; he's old enough to be your father!"

She counted to ten before she answered. "No, he isn't, but even if he were, what difference would it make? Who are you to judge whether or not I can love an older man? Court is kind, and loving—"

"And rich!" His voice quavered with anger. "That's what this is all about, isn't it? He can buy you everything you ever wanted, keep you in comfort, even luxury."

"Keep me!" She clenched her fists in an effort to control her raging temper. "You mean set me up in an apartment, buy my clothes and give me an allowance?"

He blinked. "Well...that is—"

She was too outraged to listen. "What gives you the right to come into my house and insult me? Worse, how can you stand there and besmirch your father's character that way?"

He looked surprised. "I didn't—"

"Oh, yes you did. He has too much respect for you and Noelle, and for your mother's memory, to keep a succession of women just to satisfy his physical urges."

John's face turned scarlet and he bolted out of the chair. "That's not what I meant!" he shouted. "It's your morals I'm questioning, not his."

"Oh?" She was as dangerously calm as he was violent. "You mean it's okay for a man to keep a woman—after all boys will be boys—but a kept woman is automatically a tramp?"

If she hadn't been so furious she would have been amused at the frustration that twisted his face. He looked as if he were about to explode as he stomped across the room toward the door.

"It's a waste of time talking to you. You won't even try to understand."

Kirsten practically flew off the sofa and managed to reach the door before he did, then planted herself in front of it so he couldn't get out without forcibly moving her.

"You're wrong, John," she said breathlessly. "I'll make every effort to understand your objections if you'll just talk rationally and stop insulting me. I love him. Why do you find that so hard to believe? You love him, don't you?"

He was breathing heavily, too. "Of course. He's my father," he snapped.

"But that's not the only reason, is it?" If she could just get the conversation on a more even keel maybe they'd both calm down and try to understand each other.

He paused a moment. "No, I love him because he's a great guy. He's always there when I need him and he cares about me."

Kirsten nodded. "Those are some of the same reasons I love him, and neither age nor wealth has anything to do with it."

He looked skeptical, and she knew she was going to have to work at convincing him. "Please don't leave. Stay and I'll fix lunch. Do you like cold turkey sandwiches?"

"Well, I . . . I don't think . . ."

She took his arm and urged him toward the small dining room. "Please, John. Won't you just give me a chance? Who knows, you might even find that you don't dislike me so much after all."

She gave him her most appealing smile. "I'll even let you help make the sandwiches. Which do you prefer, mayonnaise or mustard?"

He let her lead him into the kitchen, where they worked side by side slicing turkey and stacking it on slices of bread.

While they ate at the round linen-covered table, she asked him how he liked it at Yale.

At first she had to draw the answers out of him, but slowly he warmed to her questions and told her about his studies and his classmates. He even touched on some of the hell-raising they'd indulged in.

It wasn't until after she'd cleared away the food and they were lingering over cappuccino that Kirsten again raised the explosive subject of her relationship with Court. "Johnny, did you bother to check out my background before you started forming opinions about me?"

For a moment the look on his face told her that for a short time he'd forgotten their original discussion, and she was genuinely sorry when his features closed against her. "No, I heard all I needed to know." His tone was cold.

Her eyebrows quirked. "Oh, then you know who my parents are?"

"Your parents? Noelle didn't mention your parents. Why should she?"

So she'd been right. John only knew what Noelle had chosen to tell him about her. Court probably hadn't had the time or the privacy to discuss her with his son yet.

"Because by not doing so she allowed you to form a wrong opinion," Kirsten answered. "My father is Dane Anderson, and he and his family have owned and operated Anderson Realty, the largest privately owned real estate company in the area, for three generations. Also, my mother, Helen, is a partner in one of the most prestigious law firms in Northern California. We have more money than we can possibly spend, Johnny, and part of it is mine in my own right."

Kirsten hated talking about her family's wealth. It was a subject that none of them ever discussed with anyone but their bankers and investment counselors. Also, she'd never before been so crass as to point out that it was old money, three generations old. Not nouveau riche like the Forresters'.

She ignored John's obvious dismay as she continued, "I've always had everything I wanted that money can buy. My father saw to that, but you can't buy love, and that's all I want from Court."

Chapter Ten

Kirsten had been watching John Forrester's expressions turn from smug to surprised to dismayed. He stood up so quickly that his chair fell over, and he turned to retrieve it. "I'll kill that sister of mine," he threatened darkly.

"Don't be too hard on Noelle," Kirsten said. "She sees me as a double threat. She and your dad have been very close since your mother died. She's dependent and possessive of him. It galls her that the 'other woman' in his life is only four years older than she. I'm quite sure I'd react the same way if I were her."

John sank back down in the chair. "Are you going to marry Dad?" he asked tonelessly.

"I'm afraid Noelle has taken my romance with your father several steps further in her mind than he has," she answered ruefully. "There's been no talk of marriage."

John looked at her. "Is he in love with you?"

Kirsten shrugged. "I'm not sure. He acts as if he is, but he fights against his feelings for me. To be blunt, he doesn't want to get permanently involved with any woman, and especially not one the age of his children.''

''Are you . . .'' He stopped, then shook his head. ''Never mind.''

She knew what he had been about to ask, and decided it was better to tell him than to let him wonder. ''We're not sleeping together, if that's what you wanted to know.''

Again he seemed surprised at her frankness. ''Why not?'' His tone was disbelieving. ''Are you holding out for marriage?''

Her face must have revealed the storm of rage that shook her, because he quickly held up his hand in a gesture of apology. ''I'm sorry, Kirsten. I don't really believe that; it just slipped out.'' He ran his hand through his dark brown hair. ''Or maybe I do. I'm too upset to sort out my feelings. I didn't know anything about this until I came home, and then Noelle made it sound as if you'd cast some sort of spell over Dad.''

He stood up once more and turned away from her. ''To tell you the truth, I'm not sure you haven't. You've sure as hell got me confused. I don't mean to be insulting, but I just don't understand why he would be attracted to you. You're not anything like . . .''

He clamped his mouth shut before he could utter the rest of the sentence, but she heard it as clearly as if he'd said it. ''I'm not anything like your mother. That's what you were going to say, wasn't it?''

Slowly he turned back to look at her. ''Yes, it is. Mom was tiny, and blond, and wholly dependent on Dad. She dropped out of college after they were married, and she never worked outside the home. Noelle says you're a college graduate and hold a management-level position at Evergreen.''

Kirsten smiled with relief. ''I'm glad to hear that I'm not like your mother, Johnny. I'm sure she was a much nicer person than I am, but I'd never want to be a replacement for her in Court's life. He has to want me because I'm *me*, not because I remind him of the wife he lost."

John sighed. "All right, you win." He sounded resigned rather than welcoming. "I won't do anything to discourage Dad where you're concerned, but neither will I encourage him. I think you're badly mismatched, but if he wants you enough to disregard Noelle's opposition and my indifference, then I guess he could never be happy without you." John walked toward the door.

Kirsten followed. "Thank you. I can't promise that he'd never be unhappy with me, but I solemnly swear that I'll never deliberately hurt him."

John opened the door, then turned and took her hand. "Goodbye, Kirsten. It's been...interesting. See you tonight."

That evening Kirsten dressed with even more care than she'd planned. She was determined to show Court's son that she was a wealthy, intelligent woman who could take care of herself and didn't need a man to support her.

She chose a black, raw silk, fitted cocktail dress with a deeply scooped neckline, long, tight sleeves and a slender skirt that ended about two inches above the knee. Around her small waist she fitted a wide sash of bright fuchsia that was tied at the side in a magnificently oversized bow.

She'd bought the dress from a well-known designer while vacationing in France the year before, and she was quite sure that Noelle Forrester didn't have anything in her wardrobe more chic or more expensive. Under it she wore sheer black tights and nothing else.

The gown was a statement in itself and needed no embellishment, but she did wear the diamond earrings and dinner ring that had been her grandmother's. With her understated makeup featuring blusher and lipstick in the exact shade of fuchsia as her sash, and her rich brown hair swept up in a riot of ringlets on the crown of her head, she was secure in the knowledge that neither Court nor John would mistake her for a teenager tonight.

At the Forrester estate Court answered the doorbell himself. He was wearing a black suit with a white pleated shirt, and a big smile on his face.

He looked at her, then looked again as he took her hand and guided her into the foyer. "Good Lord," he murmured as his gaze roamed from her sparkling curls slowly downward to her black patent-leather spike-heeled pumps.

"You like?" she asked as she pivoted gracefully so he could appreciate the beautiful lines and perfect fit of the gown.

"Oh, yes, I like," he said, while the gleam in his eyes told her just how much he enjoyed what he saw. "But do I dare touch?"

She bridged the slight gap between them and put her arms around his neck. "You don't dare *not* touch," she whispered as his arms slid around her waist and pulled her closer.

"It's a good thing," he said, and brushed her lips with his, "because I couldn't have kept my hands off you tonight even if it meant buying you a new dress in the morning."

He found her lips again, and this time they clung, and melded, and sent unspoken messages to every area of her exuberant body. "Oh, how I've missed you these last few days." His tone was husky.

"I've missed you, too." She kissed the corners of his mouth. "Are you feeling all right now?"

He moved his lips to the side of her throat, sending tremors down her spine. "You missed your calling, sweetheart," he said tenderly. "You should have been a nurse."

"No," she murmured, "but I'll probably be a good mother. I have this compulsion to take care of those I love."

"And that includes me?" It was a question rather than a statement.

She was amazed at the sudden tension in him, as if he honestly didn't know how she'd answer.

"You most of all, Court. Don't you know that? There's so much love in me for you that I'm sure I must glow with it."

His arms tightened, and he lifted his head to look at her. "Then marry me, Kirsten."

She caught her breath as his words struck a melodious chord that vibrated through her finely tuned nervous system.

"I know we have almost nothing in common except our love for each other," he continued urgently, "but I'm not as self-sacrificing as I'd hoped I could be. I love you so much that the thought of sending you away is intolerable, although, for your own best interest, it's what I should do."

She snuggled against him. Even in her euphoric state Kirsten was aware that there were many problems that should be discussed before she committed herself to him, but she also knew she'd marry him in spite of the obstacles. She wasn't going to break the romantic spell he'd woven with his declaration of love.

"Of course I'll marry you, darling," she murmured happily. "And it will be forever. I don't ever again want to hear you talking about sending me away 'for my own good.'"

He relaxed then and laughed softly. "You won't. Once you're mine I'll never let you go. I couldn't live without you."

Their mouths met, and Kirsten felt as if she'd been born again, full-grown and filled with joy and anticipation. The excitement of the passion Court could so easily arouse in her pounded through her veins, but it was more than that. For the first time in her life she felt complete, as though she'd finally been united with a part of herself that she hadn't known was missing until this passionate, unselfish and honorable man showed her what love was all about.

When they pulled apart they were both trembling, but Court managed a playful grin. "Some Romeo I am," he grumbled. "Proposing in the hallway. I couldn't even wait to get you in a romantic setting first."

He put his arm around her waist and led her toward the sitting room where he'd taken her the first time he'd brought her to his house.

"But that's the most romantic part of all," she teased. "I love it when you lose control of your emotions with me."

He hugged her to his side. "Watch it, love," he said huskily. "As the old saying goes, 'you ain't seen nothin' yet,' and if I let go completely, we're going to miss dinner, and probably breakfast and lunch tomorrow."

Kirsten turned into his embrace, and wrinkled her nose at him. "Promises, promises," she murmured as his other arm came around her and he took her mouth in a hard, probing kiss that lit fires deep inside her.

Eventually Court was able to put her aside, but not without a tremendous effort that cost him dearly. He'd forgotten how agonizing restraining passion could be for a man. Actually, he couldn't remember ever needing a woman this badly before. Not even Barbara.

As he mixed drinks for each of them with hands that shook, he was buffeted by conflicting emotions. Surprise that he'd actually proposed marriage to her. That had never been part of his plan for tonight. Although he'd dreamed of having her with him always, he'd wanted to introduce her to Johnny and straighten things out with Noelle first.

He also felt uncertain. Would a woman as young and vibrant as Kirsten really be content for long with a May-September romance? He'd known all along that such a thing was folly, but he hadn't reckoned with the intensity of his love, his need for her. Although he had no doubt about his ability to satisfy her physical needs now, could he continue to do so as the years went by?

But transcending everything else was a happiness that shimmered and glowed and reached into his very soul. He adored this beautiful, warm, compassionate sprite who became child, career woman, or seductress by simply changing her clothes. One thing was certain; she'd never bore him, and he suspected that if he could find a way to let her know the extent of his love for her, she'd give him the glimpse of heaven that few mortals are privileged to have.

Half an hour later, John was the first to join them. He, too, was wearing a dark suit, and he looked older, more mature, than his nineteen years. She noticed now that he bore a strong resemblance to his father.

Court and Kirsten both arose from the sofa where they'd been sitting, and Court beamed with pride as he introduced her to his son. Her eyes widened with surprise. Court didn't know that she and John had already met! Her gaze briefly questioned the younger man's, but his was as shocked as hers.

Then she realized that it was the way she looked that had surprised him, and her smile widened. Well, now he knew she was a woman, and sexy enough to impress any man, even his father.

Since he couldn't seem to find his voice, Kirsten spoke. "Hello, John, it's nice to see you again." She turned to look at Court. "John and I met this morning when he came to call on me."

She knew her pronouncement might cause a problem, but she wasn't going to start off their life together by lying to him.

She was right. "He what!" Court didn't sound pleased.

This time it was John who spoke. "I went to see Kirsten this morning, Dad. Sorry, I should have told you. We had a talk and she invited me to stay for lunch."

Court looked from John to Kirsten. "I see." His voice was tight. "And what did you talk about?"

Her stomach knotted, but Johnny answered calmly. "I accused her of being interested only in your money, and she let me have it with both barrels." He grinned. "By the time we got through shouting at each other we had the whole thing out in the open. She says she loves you very much, and I believe her."

Kirsten could see by his expression that Court was furious, but before she could intervene he roared, "Who gave you the right to pry into my private affairs and insult—"

She caught him by the arm and dug her fingers into his biceps in an effort to get his attention. "Court, please! It's all right!"

He turned his gaze on her. "It's not all right," he said angrily. "I won't have him—"

She raised her voice. "Please, darling, listen to me! It was a fair shouting match. I said some nasty things to him, too. Remember, I can fight my own battles."

His muscles under her palm flexed, but his expression softened a bit and he put his arm around her and drew her to him. "Honey, it's not only my right but my duty to discipline my son."

"Fine," she said, and melted against him. "Have at him all you want, but not over me. I'd kind of hoped he'd learn to like me."

Court put his other arm around her, and looked over the top of her head at John. "I'm going to marry her, Johnny." His tone was calmer. "I asked her a few minutes ago and she did me the incredible honor of saying yes. Don't spoil our happiness tonight."

Kirsten had her face buried in Court's shoulder and couldn't see John, but when he spoke his tone was also calm. "Congratulations, Dad. When I saw Kirsten this morning she was wearing jeans and a sweatshirt and looked like a kid. Frankly, I couldn't imagine what attracted you to her, but when I walked in here just now and saw her like this..." He paused. "Well, let's just say I hope the two of you will be very happy."

Court released Kirsten and hugged his son, and she hoped Johnny would see the gratitude that she couldn't put into words, but knew must be plainly visible on her face.

He did, and took both of her hands. "Just one thing," he said in an uncharacteristically shy tone. "Do I have to call you Mommy?"

She whooped with laughter and swung playfully at him as he snatched her up in his arms and hugged her, too, but when he released her his merriment was gone.

"Dad," he said hesitantly, "if you don't mind some well-meant advice, I'd like to suggest that you don't mention your engagement to Noelle tonight. It would be better if you could tell her tomorrow when you can be alone with her. She'll cause a scene and... well... it's just better if..."

Court nodded. "You're right, son. Thanks for pointing it out. I'll wait and talk to her tomorrow."

Noelle arrived a short time later. Court had mentioned that she was again staying at the sorority house after spending several days at home while he was ill.

Tonight she looked glamorous in a miniskirted dress of holly-berry-red taffeta and matching strap sandals. With it she wore a ruby choker necklace and earrings, but when she saw Kirsten there was envy in her deep blue eyes. "I'd kill for a dress like that," she said. "Where did you get it?"

Kirsten told her but added, "You don't need a dress like mine; the one you're wearing is just right for you. You look beautiful, Noelle."

Court's daughter brightened and seemed surprisingly pleased with the compliment. For the first time Kirsten realized that Noelle wasn't as sure of herself as she seemed. Could her outward bluster be a front to hide her inner insecurity?

Kirsten had been dreading this dinner with Court's son and daughter, but much to her surprise it turned out to be an enjoyable evening. Although Johnny had taken the abrupt news of her engagement to his father with good grace, she knew that his original statement to her still stood. He thought she and Court were mismatched and that marriage between them would be a mistake. However, he cared enough about his father not to voice his opinion, and for that she was grateful.

Also, he'd apparently had a talk with Noelle because she curbed her petulance and displayed a keen intelligence and a delightful sense of humor.

Kirsten began to hope that she and Court's daughter could eventually learn to get along, after all.

John excused himself at ten, pleading a late date, and mentioned that he wouldn't be coming back home that night. Court frowned his disapproval but, much to Kirsten's relief, he didn't voice it.

Noelle left a few minutes later, and when the door shut behind her Court took Kirsten in his arms and kissed her. "I should get a medal for endurance," he murmured. "Have you any idea how hard it's been to keep my hands off you for the past three hours?"

She nuzzled his throat. "You caressed my knee under the table during dessert," she reminded him huskily.

He chuckled. "Yeah, but I quickly got in such a state that I didn't dare stand up, so I had to stop."

She felt herself blush as he loosened his hold so they could move. "Come with me," he said softly, and walked arm in arm with her up the winding staircase.

Her heart pounded with anticipation while her stomach knotted with wariness. She wanted him so much, but he was a lover of longtime experience, and she was a novice. Could she please him? Could she trust her instincts? Or would she panic and do everything wrong? Would he tell her what he wanted, or would he be upset because she was too inexperienced to know?

He opened a door to reveal a small, comfortably furnished sitting room, with a glimpse of a large bedroom on the other side of a wide archway. He looked at her and smiled. "Those rooms downstairs are so open and the carpet so thick that I never know when someone's going to walk in and take me by surprise."

She had the impression of color in shades of green and gold and brown plus a crackling fire in the fireplace as he took her to the couch. He removed his suit coat and sat down with her. "I don't want any surprises tonight," he said, and then she was again in his arms, and the only thing that mattered was the flexing of his muscular thighs against her lightly clad bottom as he pulled her onto his lap.

His open mouth covered hers while one hand moved slowly up her leg and the other one cupped her breast. She was being ignited from all angles, and she clutched at his hair with her fists as she parted her lips and with a low moan of desire welcomed the intimacy of his probing tongue.

His hand moved to her zipper, and she felt the pull as it parted to reveal her bare back. Shivering with pleasure, she shifted unconsciously as he caressed her nude flesh, then shifted again when his fingers teased her nipple.

The hand on her thigh tightened as he muttered agonizingly, "Sweetheart, sit still. I can only stand so much of that."

For a moment she didn't understand what he meant, then she realized he was talking about the way she moved back and forth in his lap. Her first reaction was alarm, and she sat up. "I'm sorry, did I hurt you?"

He seemed puzzled for a moment, then his expression changed to amazement. "No, you didn't hurt me," he said. "Kirsten, are you a virgin?"

She felt the confounded blush again and looked away. Now she'd ruined everything. He'd be more certain than ever that she was too young and naive for him.

Her face flamed as she nodded. "Yes." It was little more than a whisper. "I'm sorry."

His expression changed again, this time from amazement to wonder. "Sorry?" he answered softly. "Oh, my darling, don't you know what a precious gift you've brought me?"

He pulled her down into his embrace again, but this time he was gentle, almost fearful. "Every man dreams of being the first to make love to the woman he married," he said against her hair, "but there aren't many twenty-five-year-old virgins around anymore."

She burrowed her face in his chest self-consciously. "I know. It's not that no man ever wanted me. Quite a few have, but none of them lived up to my ideals."

He nuzzled her cheek with his lips. "And I do?"

"Oh, my, yes," she said enthusiastically as she lifted her head. "I've always known that I couldn't refuse you anything if you really wanted me."

He hugged her close. "If I wanted you?" His tone was ragged. "Oh God, Kirsten, I've been nearly out of my mind with wanting you. I love you. I love you so much."

His voice broke, and she could tell from the raspiness of his breathing that he was struggling for control.

She stroked his head and thrilled at the happiness that radiated through her in waves so fierce that it was almost more than she could bear. Would Court ever truly understand the depth of her love for him?

Yes, he will, she vowed, *because I'll spend the rest of my life showing him.*

They were still sitting there in the tangled intimacy of their embrace, one of his hands cupping her bare breast under her unzipped dress and the other one inching its way up under her short skirt, when there was a soft knock on the unlocked door.

Before either of them could move, it swung open and Noelle's voice called, "Daddy, I forgot to pick up my mink coat earlier so I came back..."

The resulting silence built second by second until it became a roar.

Chapter Eleven

Noelle's face was white, her features slack and her lovely eyes huge with shock. Kirsten felt as if she'd sustained a blow and had the breath knocked out of her, and Court had the guilty look of a man caught in an extramarital affair.

The impressions were fleeting, formed in a matter of seconds, but firmly branded in Kirsten's psyche. She was the first to react, and she scrambled to get off Court's lap. She clutched at her dress.

Court grabbed for her, but she eluded him. Quickly she fumbled with the long, inconvenient back zipper.

"Dammit, Noelle," Court roared. "What gives you the right to come bursting into my private rooms—"

"How could you?" Noelle's voice was low, but the anguish in it cut across Court's and left him speechless.

"How could you bring *her* here to Mama's house? To the bedroom you and Mama shared?"

Distraught though Kirsten was, she could see that this was no act.

Court stood and straightened his clothes. When he spoke again his voice was calm. "I'm your father, Noelle. I don't have to answer to you. Your mother's been gone for over three years. We've got to get on with our lives."

He'd been approaching her as he spoke, but when he tried to take her in his arms she lashed out at him. "Leave me alone," she cried. "I don't think you ever loved Mama. If you had you couldn't be making a fool of yourself with a younger, more beautiful woman now that she's gone. You don't need me or Johnny anymore. All you care about is Kirsten!"

A sob shook her, and only then did she let her father hold her, comfort her.

Kirsten was trembling with shock and distress, and for the first time she realized that her face was also wet with tears. She had to get out of there. It had finally dawned on her that she was the intruder. The best thing she could do for all concerned was to leave and put an end to this fiasco.

Quietly she walked out.

Kirsten went home that night only long enough to throw a few things in a duffel bag, then left again to drive to the Santa Cruz Mountains on the coast. She wouldn't be able to sleep anyway, and she had to have some time to herself.

When she was in college, her dad had given her a small two-room cabin nestled in a grove of pine trees not far from the campus. She and her friends had used it, sometimes to party, often for quiet weekends, but she'd also loved to go there by herself just to think.

She'd learned to know herself well during those sessions. Since becoming involved with Court, she'd lost the ability to reconcile her needs and her limitations. She needed him, but it was plain now that she couldn't have him without shattering his loving relationship with his son and daughter. She wouldn't do that. She loved him too much to cause him that kind of anguish.

Court studied his face in the mirror as he shaved. He'd have sworn that he'd aged ten years in the past thirty-six hours. His features were pale and pinched, and there were deep blue circles under the eyes that still mirrored his torment.

Unplugging his electric razor, he turned on the water in the sink. He was just too damn old for these wild emotional roller-coaster rides! In the space of seconds he'd been plunged from euphoria to sheer hell, and sometime during the tumult that followed, Kirsten had slipped away from him again.

He rubbed his hand over his face in a gesture of despair. She hadn't returned to her condominium, but at least he knew she was all right. He'd contacted her parents, who admitted she'd been in touch with them, but at her request they refused to tell him where she was.

After living in that hell for two nights and a day, he knew what he had to do.

He'd been faced with an impossible dilemma, a choice between his daughter and the woman he loved. No man should have to make that decision. Either way he'd lose, but if it had to be done, there was only one way he could go and still save his sanity. Even so, it would always haunt him.

As he dressed in clean jeans and a sweatshirt, his tired mind reviewed once more the events of that Friday night. When he'd realized that Kirsten was gone, and Noelle's hysteria showed few signs of abating, he'd summoned the doctor. After being given a sedative she'd slept, and Court had started trying to contact Kirsten, but to no avail.

On Saturday he'd sought emergency counseling for both Noelle and himself from a noted family counselor who was a good friend. He'd assured Court that Noelle's behavior was a normal mixture of jealousy toward a rival for her father's attention, fear of the changes taking place in her life, over which she had no control, and unresolved grief over her mother's death.

"She's a strong-willed young woman, Court," he'd said. "She'll dominate you if she can. Don't let her do it. Be kind and loving, but let her know that you won't be intimidated."

His eyes had twinkled as he stood up, signifying the end of their session. "Then try to remember that the same thing applies to her. She's a woman, my friend, so stand aside and let her find her own way. She'll be a better person for it."

Now, at ten o'clock on Sunday morning, he was preparing to tell his daughter the decision he'd made. Then he was going to Kirsten's parents to make them tell him where she was. He was past caring what methods he had to use to do it.

Noelle was dressed and sitting curled up at one end of the love seat, watching television when Court walked into her room. She looked up and smiled, and he was reminded of the happy little girl who used to run to him with her arms outstretched every time he came home.

"Hello, Daddy," she said, and put her feet on the floor. He leaned down to kiss her, then seated himself beside her.

"Hello, sweetheart. Did you sleep well last night?"

She nodded. "Yes, I feel much better today."

She looked better. The lines of strain were gone from her face, and her delicate coloring had come back. She seemed much more relaxed and in control.

He took a deep breath and turned to her. "Noelle, you and I need to talk about what happened the other night."

Her smile disappeared and she looked away. "I know." Her tone was barely audible. "I'm sorry for the way I behaved. It was . . . it was just as if something snapped . . ."

Court took her hand. "I know, baby. I understand how difficult it is for you to let your mother go. As long as everything stays the same, it's easy to believe that she's not dead, but just gone away. That maybe she'll come back. I deluded myself that way for a long time, too."

Noelle turned her startled gaze on him. "You did?"

"Yes, I did. For a while that was the only way I could stand the loss. But eventually you have to face reality or you'll be stuck in a time warp, unable to move forward and grow with the years. Barbara wouldn't have wanted that for you. She was a loving, generous woman. She hoped you'd have a full and happy life, and she'd have wanted the same for me."

Noelle's face clouded. "I want that for you, Dad, but why does it have to be with Kirsten? Why can't it be a woman your own age?"

Court was careful not to let his impatience with her show. "I don't know why," he said carefully. "Heaven knows I wouldn't have chosen to fall in love with a woman nearly half my age, but I did, and I'm not going to give her up. You're twenty-one years old, honey. Next spring you'll graduate from college and then you'll be on your own. You've already moved away from me. So has Johnny. I'm alone in this big house, and I'm lonely."

"But I could move back—"

"No." His tone was adamant. "You have your own life to live, and I have mine. There'll be no moving back, either literally or figuratively."

He hesitated, wishing with all his heart that he could spare his daughter the pain he was going to inflict, but knowing it had to be done, for her sake as well as his own.

"Noelle, there's something you have to know. I've asked Kirsten to marry me and she said she would."

Noelle gasped, but Court continued. "The wedding will take place as soon as we can arrange it, and I'm making plans to be gone for six months on an extended honeymoon. I'm sorry if this upsets you. I'd very much like for you to be pleased for me, but with or without your approval, I'm going to make Kirsten my wife."

Kirsten returned from her walk among the giant coastal redwoods in the beautiful Santa Cruz Mountains as the sun was setting in the late Sunday afternoon. The soft breeze off the ocean was chilly even through the red quilted parka she wore over her jeans and turquoise sweater.

She'd managed to find a measure of peace in the two days she'd been staying at the cabin. The isolation of the area, plus the lack of television or even a radio, gave her plenty of time to ponder. It hadn't brought the answers she wanted, but she'd gained the strength to do what she perceived as best for Court and his family.

Best for her, too, because she couldn't be happy if the man she loved was constantly torn between his passion for her and his paternal bond with his children.

The tiny cottage came into view, and she felt a touch of sadness. In just a few hours, after the traffic that jammed the highway between Santa Cruz and San Jose had thinned, she'd have to leave this secluded haven and return to the city, and to the heartache that waited for her there.

Inside, Kirsten built a fire in the wood-burning potbellied stove and put the heavy old tea kettle filled with water on top to heat for tea. She hadn't had the electricity turned on, but relied on battery-operated lanterns for light. Her meals consisted mostly of cold cuts, fruit and vegetables.

She'd just washed the last bite of her pita sandwich down with a swallow of tea when she heard a car coming up the rutted lane that led from the state road to the cabin. A cold rush of fear immobilized her for a moment as she remembered that she was alone with no close neighbors in the area.

Quickly she shut off the lantern that was on the table, then took it with her as she hurried over to make sure that the door was locked and bolted.

It was secure, and as she moved to the window to look out, she realized that there was nothing so dark as the woods at night. All she could see were the twin headlights of a car as it stopped out front.

The driver left the motor and the lights on as he got out and slammed the door behind him. The figure of a large man wearing jeans and a heavy jacket appeared briefly in the glow of the headlamps as he walked around the car toward her, then disappeared again in the darkness.

Who was he and what did he want? She hadn't seen him well enough to recognize him, but no one knew she was here.

Her heart was pounding as heavy footsteps creaked on the steps and the wooden porch. She clutched the heavy metal lantern, measuring it for use as a weapon as he tried the door, then knocked.

Her breath came in little gasps of fear as she stepped back and moved to the side so she'd be behind the door if he kicked it in.

Another knock, this one more of a bang, was accompanied by a raised voice. "Kirsten, it's Court. Are you in there?"

The rush of relief left her weak, and for a moment she leaned against the wall, but when the banging and shouting began again she quickly turned on the lantern and unbolted the door.

Court walked in without waiting for an invitation, then turned to face her. "Why were you here in the dark?" His tone was cool.

"You scared me. I heard the car and knew I was all alone up here."

"You'd have done well to have thought of that two days ago," he answered. "Excuse me while I turn off the engine."

He walked out, leaving Kirsten gaping. Her parent had apparently told him where she was, but why had he followed her? He didn't seem especially glad to see her.

She lit another lantern, and the two of them illuminated the room except for a few lingering shadows.

Court returned and took off his heavy jacket. He held a folded piece of business stationery and handed it to her. "You seem to have forgotten to mention this to me," he said.

Even without unfolding it she knew it was her resignation from Evergreen Industries. "Where did you get it?"

"Marguerite told me about it when I called her earlier to ask if she had any idea where you might be. I stopped by the plant and picked it up. Does it have anything to do with my reluctance to set up a day-care center?"

"No," she said tonelessly. "It has to do with your lack of trust in me and your indifference."

"Indifference?" The word echoed in the silent room. "My God, woman, I've been in a state of turmoil ever since I met you. It's you who's indifferent. Every time something doesn't go the way you think it should, you either clam up and refuse to discuss it, or you run away from me."

She opened her mouth to deny what he said, but the very fact that she'd spent the past two days here, hiding away instead of facing the problem with him, added weight to his argument.

"I'm sorry if that's what I've been doing," she said instead, "but when I submitted that resignation you'd disappeared and been gone for two weeks without ever attempting to get in touch with me. I thought you were on vacation. One you'd been planning all along without bothering to mention."

With a groan, Court reached for her and drew her into his arms. "You're right," he said, "my behavior was unforgivable. I can only plead temporary insanity. You do that to me, sweetheart. I love you so much, but we're such an unlikely pairing. I can't believe that you truly want me when you could have your pick of men your own age."

Kirsten snuggled against him and wondered how she'd find the strength to tell him she couldn't marry him. She didn't doubt his love for her, but was it strong enough to survive if marrying her meant losing his daughter?

"Believe it," she murmured as he melded her body to the full length of his own. "Your age isn't important, but your children are." She took a deep breath. "Court, I can't marry you knowing that Noelle is so violently opposed—"

His mouth on hers cut off her words and her train of thought. She'd missed him so much that being in his arms again was pure heaven.

"I have something to tell you," he said unsteadily a few minutes later, "and I want you to listen carefully. I love Noelle. That will never change, but you are my life, my love, my reason for living, and I've already told her that I'm going to marry you with or without her blessing."

They cuddled together on the couch, and for the next hour Court talked almost steadily, telling Kirsten everything that had happened after he'd realized she'd left the house on Friday night. He spoke in detail of his and Noelle's counseling sessions with the psychologist, the conclusion the counselor had drawn and his final showdown with his daughter.

"She's agreed to continue the counseling," he concluded. "She even admitted that her biggest reason for not wanting me to marry a younger woman is because she's afraid we'll start another family and then I won't need her and Johnny anymore."

Kirsten felt almost delirious with happiness. Court was adamant about wanting to marry her even if it meant a serious rift with his daughter. Neither she nor Noelle wanted that, and apparently Noelle was finally willing to give a little instead of always taking.

But a family...? How had he answered Noelle? "Did you reassure her?" she asked, meaning reassure her that he wouldn't have more children.

"Of course," he answered, and her euphoria faded along with her hope of bearing Court's babies. "I told her that I hadn't stopped loving her when John was born," he continued, "and that no matter how many babies you and I have, there'll be more than enough love to go around."

Kirsten whooped with joy and hugged him even closer. "Oh, my darling, I love you! I've never doubted that, and I hope you never will again. Can we be married soon?"

"We'd better be, sweetheart," he murmured huskily, "because I can't wait much longer. I'm looking forward to an extended honeymoon, and when we come back you can work with an architect to draw up plans for a new house. I'm going to ask your dad to sell the estate."

Kirsten was surprised at the wave of relief Court's announcement sent through her. It was quickly followed by uncertainty. "Darling, are you sure? What about Noelle and John? They won't—"

His hand under her sweater caressed her breast. "If they're truly upset by the idea, I'll arrange to have it transferred to them, jointly, but you and I need our own home. You don't mind, do you?"

Her fingers inched up his jean-clad thigh. "Not at all. It's too big, and I don't care for all that glass."

Court chuckled. "My feelings exactly. By the way, I have a wedding present for you."

Her eyes widened. "A wedding present?"

He laughed. "Well, not exactly, it's more like an agreement, but I think it will make you happy. I'm going to call a meeting of my board of directors as soon as possible and propose that we set up a preschool day-care center in the new addition."

Kirsten gasped as the conflicting emotions of delight and despair tore through her.

She straightened and looked at him, but it was the despair that was mirrored in her eyes. "Why have you suddenly changed your mind, Court? Do you think that you have to bargain with me to get me to marry you?"

The shock on his face told her she'd made a serious mistake even before he spoke. "The thought never occurred to me," he said as he put her away from him and stood. "And speaking of trust, we both have some work to do in that department."

He turned from her and walked over to the stove and its fading warmth. "I've been researching the child-care situation in San Jose and the surrounding area ever since you first brought it to my attention, but it takes time. We've sent out hundreds of letters and made dozens of calls to every sector of the city. It wasn't until everything was run through the computer and tabulated that I came to the conclusion that, whether I like it or not, mothers were going to continue to have to work, and they desperately need good, reasonably priced care for their children."

He ran his hand through his hair. "My decision had nothing to do with my feelings for you, but I'll admit I was happy that I could please you."

Kirsten felt awful. Once more she'd been too quick to make an assumption. She was beginning to see that this was an undesirable trait she'd have to get rid of. It was easy to point out Noelle's faults, but she'd do better to work on her own.

She got off the couch and walked over to where Court stood facing away from her. Putting her arms around his waist, she leaned her face against his back. "I'm sorry," she said softly. "I behave like a spoiled brat sometimes, but I do love you so very much."

Her hands moved under his sweatshirt, and he sucked in his breath as they made contact with his bare belly.

"You have pleased me," she continued. "I'm delighted that you're going ahead with the day-care center, but I wouldn't have thought any less of you if you'd decided not to."

Her wandering hands moved up to tangle her fingers in the hair on his chest, and he leaned back harder into her breasts and stomach, sending spirals of pleasure spinning through her.

"I didn't mention my resignation because there never seemed to be a good time to do it, but I hope you'll understand when I tell you that I'm not going to withdraw it."

He put his hands back to clutch her hips and draw her closer against his buttocks. "Why?"

She kissed his shoulder blade. "Because if I'm going to be your wife I don't think it's a good idea for me to work for you. Besides, I just want to be Mrs. Courtney Forrester, housewife, for a while before we start that family."

Her hands dipped downward and her fingers slipped under the waistband of his jeans.

With a gasp he clasped her hands with his own to still them. "Sweetheart, unless you want the first baby conceived right here on the floor of this cabin, you'd better use a little discretion," he muttered raggedly, then turned around and took her in his arms.

She was long past discretion as she raised her face to his.

"The floor's pretty hard, but I have a nice soft bed in the bedroom if you're interested."

His arms tightened as his mouth captured hers in a kiss that told her better than any words could that he definitely was.

*   *   *   *   *

COMING NEXT MONTH

#658 A WOMAN IN LOVE—Brittany Young
When archaeologist Melina Chase met the mysterious Aristo Drapano aboard a treasure-hunting ship in the Greek isles, she knew he was her most priceless find....

#659 WALTZ WITH THE FLOWERS—Marcine Smith
When Estella Blaine applied for a loan to build a stable on her farm, she never expected bank manager Cody Marlowe to ask for her heart as collateral!

#660 IT HAPPENED ONE MORNING—Jill Castle
A chance encounter in the park with free-spirited dog trainer Collier Woolery had Neysa Williston's orderly heart spinning. Could he convince her that their meeting was destiny?

#661 DREAM OF A LIFETIME—Arlene James
Businessman Dan Wilson needed an adventure and found one in the Montana Rockies with lovely mountain guide Laney Scott. But now he wanted her to follow his trail....

#662 THE WEDDING MARCH—Terry Essig
Feisty five-foot Lucia Callahan had had just about enough of tall, protective men, and she set out to find a husband her own size...but she couldn't resist Daniel Statler—all six feet of him!

#663 NO WAY TO TREAT A LADY—Rita Rainville
Aunt Tillie was at it again, matchmaking between her llama-ranching nephew, Dave McGraw, and reading teacher Jennifer Hale. True love would never be the same again!

AVAILABLE THIS MONTH:

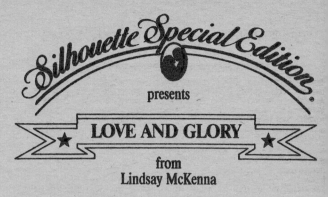

Silhouette Special Edition

presents

LOVE AND GLORY

from
Lindsay McKenna

Introducing a gripping new series celebrating our men—and women—in uniform. Meet the Trayherns, a military family as proud and colorful as the American flag, a family fighting the shadow of dishonor, a family determined to triumph—with
LOVE AND GLORY!

June: **A QUESTION OF HONOR** (SE #529) leads the fast-paced excitement. When Coast Guard officer Noah Trayhern offers Kit Anderson a safe house, he unwittingly endangers his own guarded emotions.

July: **NO SURRENDER** (SE #535) Navy pilot Alyssa Trayhern's assignment with arrogant jet jockey Clay Cantrell threatens her career—and her heart—with a crash landing!

August: **RETURN OF A HERO** (SE #541) Strike up the band to welcome home a man whose top-secret reappearance will make headline news . . . with a delicate, daring woman by his side.

"GIVE YOUR HEART TO SILHOUETTE" SWEEPSTAKES
OFFICIAL RULES
NO PURCHASE NECESSARY TO ENTER OR RECEIVE A PRIZE

To enter and join the Silhouette Reader Service, rub off the concealment device on all game tickets. This will reveal the potential value for each Sweepstakes entry number and the number of free book(s) you will receive. Accepting the free book(s) will automatically entitle you to also receive a free bonus gift. If you do not wish to take advantage of our introduction to the Silhouette Reader Service but wish to enter the Sweepstakes only, rub off the concealment device on tickets #1-3 only. To enter, return your entire sheet of tickets. Incomplete and/or inaccurate entries are not eligible for that section or section (s) of prizes. Not responsible for mutilated or unreadable entries or inadvertent printing errors. Mechanically reproduced entries are null and void.

Either way, your Sweepstakes numbers will be compared against the list of winning numbers generated at random by computer. In the event that all prizes are not claimed, random drawings will be made from all entries received from all presentations to award all unclaimed prizes. All cash prizes are payable in U.S. funds. This is in addition to any free, surprise or mystery gifts that might be offered. The following prizes are awarded in this sweepstakes:

(1)	*Grand Prize	$1,000,000	Annuity
(1)	First Prize	$35,000	
(1)	Second Prize	$10,000	
(3)	Third Prize	$5,000	
(10)	Fourth Prize	$1,000	
(25)	Fifth Prize	$500	
(5000)	Sixth Prize	$5	

*The Grand Prize is payable through a $1,000,000 annuity. Winner may elect to receive $25,000 a year for 40 years, totaling up to $1,000,000 without interest, or $350,000 in one cash payment. Winners selected will receive the prizes offered in the Sweepstakes promotion they receive.
Entrants may cancel the Reader Service privileges at any time without cost or obligation to buy (see details in center insert card).

Versions of this Sweepstakes with different graphics may be offered in other mailings or at retail outlets by Torstar Corp. and its affiliates. This promotion is being conducted under the supervision of Marden-Kane, Inc., an independent judging organization. By entering this Sweepstakes, each entrant accepts and agrees to be bound by these rules and the decisions of the judges, which shall be final and binding. Odds of winning are dependent upon the total number of entries received. Taxes, if any, are the sole responsibility of the winners. Prizes are nontransferable. All entries must be received by March 31, 1990. The drawing will take place on April 30, 1990, at the offices of Marden-Kane, Inc., Lake Success, N.Y.

This offer is open to residents of the U.S., Great Britain and Canada, 18 years or older, except employees of Torstar Corp., its affiliates, and subsidiaries, Marden-Kane, Inc. and all other agencies and persons connected with conducting this Sweepstakes. All federal, state and local laws apply. Void wherever prohibited or restricted by law.

Winners will be notified by mail and may be required to execute an affidavit of eligibility and release that must be returned within 14 days after notification. Canadian winners will be required to answer a skill-testing question. Winners consent to the use of their name, photograph and/or likeness for advertising and publicity in conjunction with this and similar promotions without additional compensation. One prize per family or household.

For a list of our most current major prizewinners, send a stamped, self-addressed envelope to: WINNERS LIST, c/o MARDEN-KANE, INC., P.O. BOX 701, SAYREVILLE, N.J. 08871

Sweepstakes entry form is missing, please print your name and address on a 3" ×5" piece of plain paper and send to:

In the U.S.	In Canada
Sweepstakes Entry	Sweepstakes Entry
901 Fuhrmann Blvd.	P.O. Box 609
P.O. Box 1867	Fort Erie, Ontario
Buffalo, NY 14269-1867	L2A 5X3

LTY-S69R

You'll flip . . . your pages won't!
Read paperbacks *hands-free* with

Book Mate • I

The perfect "mate" for all your romance paperbacks
Traveling • Vacationing • At Work • In Bed • Studying
• Cooking • Eating

Perfect size for all standard paperbacks, this wonderful invention makes reading a pure pleasure! Ingenious design holds paperback books OPEN and FLAT so even wind can't ruffle pages — leaves your hands free to do other things. Reinforced, wipe-clean vinyl-covered holder flexes to let you turn pages without undoing the strap . . . supports paperbacks so well, they have the strength of hardcovers!

Pages turn WITHOUT opening the strap.

SEE-THROUGH STRAP

Reinforced back stays flat.

Built in bookmark

BOOK MARK

BACK COVER HOLDING STRIP

10" x 7¼ . opened.
Snaps closed for easy carrying, too

Available now. Send your name, address, and zip code, along with a check or money order for just $5.95 + .75¢ for postage & handling (for a total of $6.70) payable to Reader Service to:

Reader Service
Bookmate Offer
901 Fuhrmann Blvd.
P.O. Box 1396
Buffalo, N.Y. 14269-1396

Offer not available in Canada
*New York and Iowa residents add appropriate sales tax.

BM-G